The Sheikh's L Lov

By Leslie North

The Sharqi Sheikhs Series

Book 1

<u>Blurb</u>

American tutor Kim Atkins is teaching English to a young Middle Eastern prince, but she's having a hard time keeping her eyes off his older brother. With Karim's stacked muscles and handsome face, it's hard not to be distracted. It's too bad he's rude, arrogant and very traditional, but that only makes it easier to focus on her student and the girls at the local orphanage. Besides, with glamorous beauties eager for Karim's attention, clumsy Kim could never compare.

Karim Sharqi is knee-deep in paperwork after taking over the family jewel company, but asking for help from his brother's pretty tutor goes against everything his father taught him. Karim's known from a young age that you should never rely on a woman—especially a Western woman. Her modern attitude flies in the face of his traditional values, and yet, her beauty and shy smile are proving to be an irresistible temptation.

Can two people from such different worlds ever find a common future?

Thank you for downloading 'The Sheikh's Unforgettable Lover (The Sharqi Sheikhs Series Book 1)'

Get <u>FIVE</u> full-length, highly-rated Leslie North Novellas <u>FREE</u>!

Sign-up to her mailing list and start reading them within minutes:

http://leslienorthbooks.com/sign-up-for-free-books/

Dedications

I dedicate this book to you, my loyal readers. Thank you for all the lovely e-mails, reviews, and support. Without you, this wouldn't be possible.

I'd also like to say a special thank you to *Leslie's Lovelies* who have had a huge role in making this book – you're the best! THANK YOU for all your support.

If you'd like to join Leslie's Lovelies and get exclusive advanced review copies of my latest books, please check out the Official Page here: http://leslienorthbooks.com/about/leslies-lovelies/

Contents

Chapter One

Kim Atkins watched Sheik Karim Sharqi lift free weights on the courtyard below her, sweat glistening off his body in the intense sunlight. Staring down at him, she had never seen a man so strong, so muscular, so alluring, as she imagined that perfect body pressed against hers, his hands holding her waist as she stroked his rippling muscles.

Kim turned her head to see three maids watching him from a distance. One of them was fanning herself as they whispered and giggled amongst themselves. Kim did not blame them -- Karim Sharqi was a very attractive man.

Closing her eyes, she imagined herself looking into his eyes, his dark hair neatly framing his face as his brown eyes smiled down at her. In her mind, she fisted her hand to keep from touching his perfectly straight nose perched atop luscious lips that invited her to lean in for a kiss.

She briefly wondered what his stubble would feel like rubbing against her fevered skin, as he kissed his way down her body. She swayed slightly on her feet as her all too active imagination made her body tingle at the thought of his touch.

"Does this sentence make sense?" Amare asked, interrupting her daydream.

"Huh?" Kim snapped out of her thoughts and returned her attention to Amare. She had forgotten where she was and what she was doing. "Sorry, show me," she said and took the notebook from him.

Kim had originally come to Saudi Arabia as an ESL (English as Second Language) teacher and when her contract was over, she was fortunate enough to be hired as a private tutor for Amare, the youngest son of Sheik Saeed Sharqi.

"Well done," Kim said, as she handed the notebook back to him.

"Thanks."

"You're doing really well, Amare."

"Really? I am?"

Kim grinned at him, tousling his hair, "Yes, you are."

"Cool. Father expects me to excel on all my exams," he told her as he squeezed the notebook before setting it down.

"I have no doubt that you will." Kim smiled at the young sheik. She was impressed with how hard he was working. When she had first accepted the job, she did not expect to meet such a serious student. In her experience, children born with silver spoons in their mouths tended not to work very hard.

"Not only should I work hard, I should be top of my class," Amare said solemnly.

Kim raised her eyebrows. "That is a lot of pressure."

"My father wants nothing but the best."

Kim sighed. She had heard that the Sheik was strict but she could not believe how much pressure he was putting on his son. She was glad that she had not been raised with that much expectation to do well in school. She flipped open her folder and pulled out a poem.

"We'll do the best we can," she said, handing him a sheet of paper. "See if you can interpret this poem for me."

"Sure."

Whilst Amare was reading the poem, Kim's gaze travelled back to the courtyard below. Karim was still outside in the courtyard working out and was currently doing push-ups on the slate tiled floor. The muscles in his back tensed up as he bent his arms and slowly lowered himself down.

He had taken off his shirt and his torso was bathed in sweat as Kim contemplated licking the salty sweat from his chest. Lost in thought, she watched as he reached for a towel and slowly dried the sweat from his body leaving Kim to wonder what it would feel like to stroke her fingers along those rock hard abs.

A noise from behind her made her jump as she finally realised that Karim was looking straight at her with a smirk on his face. She gasped and looked away quickly.

"Crap," she muttered under her breath.

Chapter Two

She could not believe that she had been caught staring. She tucked a lock of brown hair behind her ear and returned her attention back to Amare, where it should have been in the first place.

Don't look outside; Kim told herself. She was there to do a job and that was to tutor Amare, and not to stare at his handsome older brother. As hard as it was, she had to control herself. It was bad enough that she had been caught.

A maid knocked on the door before walking in carrying a tray of freshly made iced tea, homemade pastries, fresh fruit and cheese. She approached Kim and Amare who were studying by the window.

"Sorry to interrupt," the maid said as she placed the tray on a glass table with white marble legs. Everything in the Sharqi house was expensive. That one table was probably enough to cover Kim's monthly rent.

"Thank you," Amare said to the maid.

"Would you like anything else?"

"No, that will be all."

The maid bowed her head before she left the room. Amare gestured for Kim to eat something as he reached for his favourite pastry. She smiled and nodded. She found herself getting very thirsty due to the dry heat of Saudi Arabia. She took a sip of her iced tea and listened to Amare interpreting the poem she had given him.

"Good," she said to him. "From that poem, write a small essay, no more than a page. Analyse the register, dialect and personification used in the poem."

Amare looked from Kim back to the poem, as he opened and closed his mouth, unsure what to say. Kim offered a warm smile. "You can do it," she told him. Even though the work was advanced for his age, in the short time she had been working with him, he had far surpassed her expectations as he blew through the requirements for his upcoming exams.

While she took her job seriously, Sheik Sharqi was a formidable man and she did not want to end up on his bad side as she hoped to obtain a reference from him. The fact that all his sons were brilliant and Amare was excelling academically made her job much easier, but it didn't take the pressure off her.

"I will try," he said dubiously as he set the poem back down in front of him and stared at it.

Seeing movement down below, Kim turned to see a maid approach Karim with refreshments. Handing him a fresh towel and a bottle of water, Kim watched as he twisted the cap off and tilted the bottle up to take a long drink. Stepping back to avoid being seen as he looked up toward her balcony, she openly stared at him, hoping that he couldn't see her.

A soft voice had her turning her head as she watched the maid attempt to flirt with him while he remained oblivious. After a quiet comment from him, she quickly bowed and headed back into the house with what looked to be dejection on her face.

Kim watched as he tilted the remaining water onto his head and chest before reaching for the towel. With slow precision, he rubbed the towel across his torso as Kim covered her mouth. What she wouldn't give to be the one rubbing his body with a towel, perhaps after they had passionate sex in the shower, slowly drying his body off. Her lips following the path laid by her fingers as she rubbed the water from his sexy body.

Turning his back toward her, she bit her lip as he twisted his torso and continued to wipe the sweat off. From where she was standing, he was perfect in every way as he bent down to wipe the sweat from his legs. Tossing the towel aside, he stretched his arms up, twisting his body again. Tilting back, he looked up at Kim and winked at her as she gasped in surprise.

How long had he known that she was watching, again? she wondered as she quickly stepped back away from the window.

Chapter Three

As Kim turned from the window, she found Amare staring at her with amusement on his face. "Checking out my brother?" he asked her with a cheeky grin on his face. Coughing loudly, Kim reached for her iced tea and pretended to sooth her throat as she fought to keep the blush from creeping up her face.

"I was not," she lied. She could not believe that Amare had caught her as her blush took over and her cheeks flamed red from embarrassment. Amare rocked his head back and started laughing at her as she narrowed her gaze at him. She was already embarrassed enough, he did not need to laugh so hard at her.

"Kim, you were definitely watching him, do not deny it," he teased.

"I was not. I was just staring into space." As if that made any sense but it was the only excuse, she could come up with, as she was not very good at lying. Amare still laughed at her. It was obvious that he did not believe her.

"It is alright. Most women often look at my brother lasciviously," he said. Kim's jaw hung open before she narrowed her eyes at him.

Crossing her arms, she tapped her foot as she attempted to give him a stern stare. "I was not looking at him lasciviously!" she told him. "However, that was an excellent use of one of your vocabulary words," she added drolly as he snickered in response.

"Honestly, I would be surprised if you didn't find him attractive." Amare leaned back in his leather white chair and folded his arms over his chest as he continued to smirk. "In case you haven't noticed, every female he's around seems to flirt with him."

"He's okay," Kim said vaguely, before sipping more of her iced tea, which was rapidly becoming tepid in her hot hands. She did not particularly want to discuss how attractive Karim was with his youngest brother. She took a bite out of her besbousa and chewed it slowly. She loved the taste of the honey as the sweetness exploded in her mouth with each bite. One of the best things about living in the Sharqi residence was the great food.

"My brother is a particular man," Amare told her as he sighed. Kim swallowed before speaking.

"What do you mean by that?" she asked him.

"For starters, he does not believe in love." Kim's eyes widened.

"What?" Who did not believe in love? That did not make any sense.

"While he has dated women, he refuses to commit to any one person. I would be very careful around him. He has broken a lot of hearts and doesn't stick around to mend them."

Kim stared down at the courtyard below as Karim gathered his things. *What a shame*, she thought. All of that manliness and muscle gone to waste. Hearing that he did not commit to one person simply translated to him being a player in Kim's mind. Of course, he would; why would he stick to one woman when he could have many?

"That is sad. How can one not believe in love?" Kim asked. Amare shrugged his shoulders.

"Believe me, many women are saddened by that," Amare said. "He also never brings any women home."

"So he has never brought any home?" Kim did not want to seem too interested, but she was curious. Amare shook his head. "Not even one?"

"No."

"Oh. Did something happen to him to be that way?"

Amare started laughing. "No, he was born that way."

Kim laughed at Amare's response. She could well understand if something had happened to make him behave this way. A rough break up can make a person dislike the idea of being in a committed relationship but how could he not want love or believe in it?

Kim had often been teased by her friends for being a hopeless romantic. She loved happy endings and hoped to find a good man who would love and cherish her. She held onto the dream of falling madly in love and getting married. She could not help but feel disappointed in the fact that Karim was her exact opposite.

"From the look on your face, I guess that you believe in love?" Amare asked her.

"Of course, I do."

"Women always do; at least that is what Karim says. It seems every woman he comes across falls in love with him."

Sounds like an arrogant jerk; Kim thought to herself. "I cannot see how that is the case. He is quite unfriendly." Since becoming Amare's tutor, Kim had only exchanged greetings with him, as he never seemed interested in engaging her in conversation.

"Yes, if he does not know you, then he will not converse with you," Amare said, with half a smile on his face.

"No doubt, he is a traditional man."

"Oh yes. He is much like father in that sense. They're both set in their traditional ways but as brothers go, there can be no one better," Amare said proudly. "He has always been there for both Taleb and me."

Before Kim could make a comment about that, she heard voices from the next room. She could not make out what they were saying. Curiosity got the best of her.

"Whose voices are those?" she asked Amare.

"I am not sure about all of them, but one of them belongs to Karim," he replied. Kim was already aware that Karim owned one of the voices. His voice was so deep and distinctive, she could not mistake it for anyone else but she did not say anything. Amare would only tease her for recognising his voice. She rose to her feet and walked to the shelf where Amare kept some glassware.

"What are you doing?" he asked her. Kim picked up a glass beaker and walked towards the wall.

"Nothing, just concentrate on your work," she said and giggled. She suddenly tripped and almost fell over but managed to regain her balance. Amare burst out laughing.

"You are so clumsy," he said and kept laughing as Kim laughed with him. Tripping over her feet was a frequent occurrence. She was just glad that it was Amare that had seen her and not Karim. She put the glass beaker against the wall and then put her ear against the beaker.

"You must never do this," she said to him in mock sternness, as she attempted to hide her smile.

"Well, you are doing it in front of me, which will make me want to try it too."

"No, Amare, it's naughty."

Kim squinted as she concentrated on the conversation. She wondered whom Karim was talking to and about what. Amare watched her eavesdropping.

"So what are they talking about?" he asked her.

"I don't know. I can't really hear much."

"Then that beaker method is ineffective," Amare said with conviction as Kim giggled.

"Oh no, it should work fine; the walls are too thick." She readjusted her position as Amare laughed and shook his head. "I can't hear," she said and put her finger against her lips to quiet him. Suddenly she heard the door to the room open. Gasping, she whipped her head in that direction. In doing so, she dropped the glass beaker, smashing it into pieces on the floor.

Her eyes shot up to the figure entering the room.

Chapter Four

Amare and Kim stared at the door waiting to see who it was. Kim feared that Karim had caught her trying to eavesdrop on his conversation and she sighed with relief when she saw Taleb, the middle son, walking in. He glanced down at the broken glass and let out a low chuckle.

"Good morning, Kim," Taleb greeted her with a warm smile. Kim returned his smile. He was much friendlier than Karim was and from the moment she arrived, went out of his way to make sure that she felt welcome, whereas Karim barely smiled at all.

"Hello, Taleb, how are you?" Kim asked.

"I am well, thank you," he replied to her politely. Karim was never that polite. "How is the tutoring going?"

"Kim says that I am progressing really well." Amare told him with a grin on his face. Taleb raised his eyebrows.

"Shall I trust your words, brother?"

Amare dropped his jaw as Kim laughed. "Yes, it is true. He is doing really well. He is picking up most things really quickly," she said as Taleb smiled.

"Relax, Amare. I believe you." Taleb told him. "The men in our family are very intelligent."

"Are they now?" Kim folded her arms over her chest as she looked at the two brothers.

"Yes. We are," Amare replied with a cheeky grin on his face.

"Two against one, this isn't fair," she mocked complained as the brothers both laughed.

"Okay, we will have mercy on you." Taleb winked at her, which immediately reminded her of Karim. She would swear that she had seen him wink at her whilst he was working out. The thought of it made her stomach knot up wondering what he was thinking. "But, I can't say the same for our brother," he added.

"Thank you," she said absently before she realised that he had said something else. "I'm sorry, what did you say?"

"How are you getting on with Karim?"

The timing of Taleb's question caught her off guard as she wondered if he knew that she had been spying on his brother while he was working out in the mornings. She kept a straight face hoping that her thoughts wouldn't give her away as she did not want Taleb teasing her about Karim the way Amare had done earlier.

"Fine, I guess. Considering that I can count on one hand the number of words he's said to me since I got here."

Nodding his head, "You will have to excuse him if he is unfriendly towards you. That is just the way he is," Taleb told her. "Although, admittedly, he might be ignoring you more than he normally would, as he was told not to bother you. Our brother can be a bit…anti-American. He is much like father in that he is stuck in the old ways, but at least father recognizes the need to hire quality tutors when necessary."

Kim nodded, "I understand. I'm relieved that it isn't him that I have to tutor," she joked. If she tutored him, she would never be able to concentrate. Granted, would he even accept her help? Taleb and Amare laughed.

"It is a good thing," Amare replied with a wink as Kim frowned at him, hoping that she wouldn't blush.

"Sometimes, our brother can be a dick. Just ignore him," Taleb told her as Kim raised her eyebrows. She was not expecting Taleb to refer to Karim as a dick.

"Got it," Kim replied, now worried about being caught watching him. Would he say anything to her?

"Anyway, I interrupted your session because I came to bid you both farewell."

"Already?" Amare asked.

"Yes."

"Where are you off to?" Kim asked.

"My term at Harvard is about to begin," he replied smoothly.

Kim raised her eyebrows. *Harvard!* That was impressive. Maybe it was true that the men in their family were intelligent. Not only did they have looks, but they also had brains. It was not a common combination.

"That is amazing," Kim told him.

"I did tell you about the intelligence that runs in my family," he reminded her as he smiled broadly. Kim gasped. The level of self-conceit in that family was shocking. Taleb turned on his heel and walked out leaving Kim to wonder what would happen now that he wasn't around to shield her from Karim.

Chapter Five

Later that night, Kim had just returned from a stroll post dinner. The food they served in the Sharqi household was absolutely delicious and she had difficulty putting her fork down when everything tasted so good, so she thought that a walk might help her settle her overfull stomach.

As she walked down the hall, she saw a door half open. She stopped right in front of it and looked inside. To her surprise, it was a home office -- Karim's home office.

She spied him sitting at his desk shuffling through stacks of papers. Rubbing his head in apparent agitation, he stood up abruptly and began to pace. As he made a second circuit around the room, he happened to look up and made eye contact with Kim.

She gasped, as his gaze had caught her off guard. His cold dark stare sent shivers down her spine. He did not even smile or say anything to her. He stalked towards the door as Kim resisted the urge to back away in nervousness. She thought he was coming to say something to her, and instead, he kicked the door shut.

"Taleb was right. You are a dick," she mumbled under her breath before heading back to her room. Even if he did not want to speak to her, he did not need to kick the door shut like that. It was rude. He should at least have said good night or something.

Walking into her quarters, she sighed, as she got ready for bed. She had to admit that this was the best teaching job she ever had. Not only did they pay her well, but they included both room and board. Changing into her nightgown, she climbed into her plush four-poster bed and snuggled under the covers. Yes, things could be far worse, she told herself.

As she tried to sleep, Kim found herself tossing and turning as Karim's dark eyes were imprinted in her mind. She just could not seem to forget about them. She then remembered him half-naked, working out in the courtyard as her mind wandered to how his body glistened with sweat in the early morning sun. She knew nothing good was going to come from thinking about him but she could not help it. She tossed and turned ordering sleep to come to her, but it remained elusive.

Sighing, she sat up and pulled on her robe. Maybe something to drink would help calm her down. Walking downstairs, she went to the kitchen to pour herself a glass of milk. Sipping it slowly, she wandered back towards the stairs.

As she passed Karim's office, she saw that he still had the light on. Given the time, she assumed that he had merely left it on, so she opened the door and walked inside to turn it off. She faltered when he looked at her in surprise.

"What brings you here?" he asked her. He stared at with that dark gaze again, as his eyes swept across her body taking in her attire.

Suddenly feeling foolish for barging in, "You are working quite late. Do you want any help or anything?" Kim strived to be casual but she could feel her voice failing.

"No, I am fine."

"Are you sure? I do not mind."

"I do. I prefer working alone. Leave me," he said sternly.

Kim immediately regretted her offer of help after his curt response. What was she thinking? After everything that both Amare and Taleb told her, of course, he would not want her help.

Seeing his gaze sweep across her again, Kim realized that she wasn't dressed and quickly tightened the tie on her robe. Clutching her milk glass, she nodded mutely before backing out of the room and shutting the door behind her.

Leaning against it, she kicked herself for not thinking. What must he think of her, walking in there dressed in her nightclothes? Thoughts of being just another woman throwing herself at Karim flitted across her brain as she cursed aloud. Standing tall, she downed the last of her milk, set the empty glass down on a sideboard and stalked back upstairs. She would not make that mistake again.

Chapter Six

The next day was Kim's day off and she was excited to be able to spend some time at the girls' orphanage where she tutored them in English. Having grown up in the foster care system in the States, she was lucky to have a mentor in her life that helped her find her way and encouraged her to finish school and go to college.

Even though her time here would be short, she hoped that maybe she could provide some sort of guidance to these girls. As she was on her way out, she ran into Amare and another woman. Kim smiled and greeted him.

"Hey, Kim, leaving already?" he asked her.

"Yes, I am heading over to the orphanage."

"This is Zara, Karim's PA," Amare said to her as he introduced the women. "This is Kim, my English tutor," he said to Zara.

Kim looked at Zara. She was a couple of inches taller than she was and much curvier Dressed in a black high waist skirt, a white blouse and black high heels with her jet-black hair tucked into a high ponytail and with her flawless make-up, Zara looked glamorous. She was the complete opposite of Kim.

"Hello, Zara," Kim said with a warm smile on her face.

"Hi," Zara replied flatly. Her tone was unfriendly as she slowly looked Kim up and down. It was obvious that she was studying her. Kim immediately felt awkward and unsure what to say next.

Dressed in a pair of jeans, a t-shirt and flats, which made her look significantly shorter than Zara was, Kim could see the obvious differences between the two of them. Kim rarely wore high heels and admired women who could pull it off.

When she did, it was a disaster either for her or anything she managed to crash into. She readily admitted that she liked being casual and did not bother to dress up. Mostly because she didn't know how. Her straight brown hair was held back in a band and she was told that her blue eyes were the colour of the Mediterranean Sea, although she had yet to see for herself.

While she couldn't tell how long Zara's hair was from how she wore it, she could see that it was thick as it appeared to be threatening to burst from the hairband she had wrapped around it. Her green eyes swept over Kim as if she were an item for sale.

Looking at Amare, who was looking at the two women curiously, and then back to Zara, she kept a smile on her face. "It was nice meeting you. I will see you around," she said, as she backed up and turned to leave.

The best thing for her to do was to head out. Even after she spoke, Zara did not respond to her and simply turned to watch Kim walk out. Wow, Kim thought as she headed for the door, she's the perfect employee for Karim, they can both be silent and judgmental together.

***

After Kim's lesson at the orphanage, she went to the teacher's lounge. While she appreciated the salary she earned tutoring Amare, she felt more fulfilled working with the girls and she knew that she would miss them greatly when her contract ended.

Walking into the lounge, she looked around at all the cheerful faces who looked up when she entered. The room was small and very warm, but someone had thrown the windows open and a slight breeze ruffled curtains that had seen better days.

The furniture looked as though it was assembled from discards but the brightly painted walls and the laughing voices that greeted her made it seem far more inviting than the Sharqi home.

Greeting the other teachers with enthusiasm, they responded back just as warmly.

"How is everyone?"

"Fine," Salma, one of the teachers, replied.

"How is life in the Sharqi house? Have you met the amazing Karim yet?" asked Dania, another teacher.

Amazing? Kim asked herself. The women all leaned in to her eagerly awaiting her response.

"Yes, I have met Karim," Kim answered.

"And what is he like?" Dania asked.

"There is not much to tell."

"How can there be nothing to tell?" Salma asked her.

"You are living with a handsome, attractive and successful man. There must be something to tell," Dania added as the women laughed.

"Well, I think he is quite arrogant and rude," Kim said slowly, not wanting to speak out of turn.

"Really? But he's so handsome," Dania replied with a small smile on her face.

"He is Karim Sharqi that should be enough," Salma said with conviction as Kim frowned. She and the other women were on completely different pages.

"I wish I was the one living under the same roof as him," Dania said dreamily.

"It makes no difference to me," Kim lied. It made a difference living in the same house as him. She had witnessed him working out shirtless and had not been able to keep her eyes off him. Unfortunately, she had been caught. The weird thing was that he winked at her and then was completely cold to her afterwards. He and his stuck up PA deserved each other.

"I think Karim is arrogant," said a woman that Kim didn't know. Turning, she smiled at the Caucasian woman who spoke with an American accent.

"I am glad that someone agrees," Kim replied as both women laughed.

"I'm Rene Tazeem." She extended her hand to Kim who shook it.

"I am Kim Atkins. That name, Tazeem, are you any relation to-"

"She is married to Joshua Tazeem," Dania finished for her. "Another beautiful man!"

Rene giggled and tucked a lock of hair behind her ear. Kim was surprised to find out that a member of the royal family was married to an American.

"No fair. I want to marry a sheik too," Salma said dreamily.

"You can have Karim," Kim joked.

"Oh, I would love to."

All of them laughed together. Shame he did not believe in love; Kim thought to herself.

"I am so going to miss this place and our little chats," Dania said forlornly.

"What do you mean? Are you going to leave?" Kim asked her. Dania shook her head.

"The orphanage will have to shut down because we do not have enough funds to keep it running."

Kim gasped. "But where will they go?" she asked.

"They will have to be separated and taken to different orphanages wherever there is room."

"That is not good. They at least need to be able to stay together." Kim knew from experience that growing up alone is difficult enough and these girls have been together long enough that they've come to see each other as family. To split them up now could be disastrous to their well-being. She sighed. This was not the ending she needed to her day.

"Can we talk about something less sad, like Karim Sharqi?" Dania asked with a mischievous grin on her face. Kim just laughed and shook her head.

"There is nothing to say about Karim other than he is a hard man to get along with. Much too like his father, if you ask me," Rene replied.

"There is so much to say! Imagine living under the same roof as him," Salma interjected and placed her hand on her heart. Kim could imagine. She was living under the same roof.

"Has any one of you ever met him in person?" Kim asked. Maybe if they had met him, they would rethink their impression of him.

"Only in my dreams," Dania replied, in a wistful tone as the women laughed.

Chapter Seven

Karim leaned back in his chair and closed his eyes, enjoying the feel of the air conditioning. Rubbing his head, he stared at the pile of papers strewn across his desk. Groaning, pinched the bridge of his nose and then looked back at the papers, which hadn't moved since the last time he looked at them. He had so much to do before the shareholder meeting and it was becoming overwhelming.

He had spent the last several hours reading everything they had on the larger shareholders, the previous meeting notes and what he would need for this meeting. It was not in his nature to do anything halfway and he wanted, no *needed*, everything to be perfect for this meeting.

Suddenly the door opened and Kim walked in. Karim watched her walk cautiously towards his desk. Normally, he was good at figuring women out, but Kim had been a puzzle to him from the moment he met her.

Maybe it was because she was American, although he had met the Tazeem women and, admittedly, he couldn't understand how such steadfast bachelors could fall in love.

Love was for the weak and those who didn't have shareholder meetings.

"Anyone ever tell you that it's rude to enter without permission?" he asked her as she narrowed her gaze at him.

"I'm rude? Me?" Biting down her anger, Kim took a deep breath. "One of the maids mentioned that you had missed dinner. Since I was about to grab some dinner for myself, would you like anything to eat?"

"No." He noticed that she was holding a math textbook and determined that she was probably coming back from tutoring at the orphanage. Amare had mentioned something about it but Karim had not enquired further.

"Fine," she replied, turning to leave.

"Wait. Are you good with figures?" he asked abruptly.

"Kind of." Kim nodded hesitantly.

"I have some stuff I need sorting out." That was the closest he could come to asking her for help. He was usually giving orders and demanding things. He was definitely not used to asking for help or needing it.

Crossing her arms, she looked at him, "Anyone ever tell you that it's rude not to say please?"

Staring at her, he couldn't believe her cheek as she continued to stare back. He finally managed to ground out, "Please." Nodding her head, Kim placed her book on his desk and picked up the sheets of paper to study them.

Since her head was down, he openly looked at her taking in her casual dress. Karim could tell that she had no regard for her image, as it didn't seem as if she put much effort into it. She had very long brown hair that hung straight down her back and complemented her pale complexion. She had piercing blue eyes that he found intriguing. Her figure was more boyish than womanly, but it all seemed to suit her.

"If you don't mind?" Kim asked, as she pointed to his desk.

"By all means," Karim said, pulling the chair out for her as she walked around to sit down. Grabbing a pen and a pad of paper, she began to scribble away as he watched her work out the figures.

The problem that Karim was having was that the business accounts were outdated. His father was stuck in his ways and hated change. While Karim himself was traditional in many ways; he believed that some modern conveniences were necessary, especially when running a global business. Some change was good. For example, these outdated files, it would have been good if they had been updated and put in Excel spreadsheets.

Karim was surprised that Kim was working on the documents with such ease. She did not seem to have any difficulties. Sure, he knew that she was smart; otherwise, she would have never been tutoring Amare. His family only ever hired exceptional tutors; however, he was still surprised at how quickly she worked. He caught her biting at her lower lip as his focus shifted from the ledger sheets to her lips.

Kim started explaining the formulas to him but he found himself unable to concentrate on her words. He had never noticed how full her lips were as he wondered if they were as soft as they looked. They were just so inviting. Yet, he had to decline the invitation, as hard as it was.

"Okay," Karim said as he nodded. He decided to listen to what she was actually saying instead of focusing on her lips.

"So it is simple really," she said. "It would be the same with these figures. Let me show you."

As Karim stared at Kim, he noticed that she was quite pretty. Her face had an appealing symmetry. Her skin looked so soft that he wanted to reach out and run his hand along her skin to test exactly how soft it was...

Karim shook his head. What was he thinking? Kim was Amare's tutor. Furthermore, she was a western woman. He started wondering why he was even allowing her to help him. He was fully capable of sorting everything out by himself.

"Actually, I can take it from here," he blurted out as she looked up at him in surprise. Her lips were slightly parted and her eyes were shining brightly. He knew that he was curt but he was not bothered.

"It's okay, I do not mind helping," she said.

Why was she always wanting to help him? Karim asked himself. She strolled into his office in her nightclothes the night before and offered her help. He couldn't figure out why she had offered. It was not as if he did not have things under control. He was perfectly fine doing things himself, his way, as he had always done.

"It is fine. You may leave," he dismissed her as she looked at him with her jaw hung open.

"You just asked me for help and now you are dismissing me?" She put the pen down and shook her head. "Unbelievable."

Standing up, Kim walked around his desk and stalked toward the door. Karim could not understand what was so unbelievable about that.

Just as Kim was walking out the door, she tripped on her own foot. She stumbled forward slightly but quickly righted herself and kept walking. He raised his eyebrows and shook his head. That was not the first time he had seen her tripping over her own feet and he found that it amused him.

Karim chastised himself for looking at her so lustfully. She was not his type. And while it was clear that she wanted him, he didn't want anything to do with her. He could remember her watching him while he was working out and felt his body grow warm at her interest. Shaking himself, even if she wanted him to, he was not going to take her. Because of her, Amare was doing better than he ever had before. She was needed as his brother's tutor. Complications from an amorous female that he paid too much attention to, he did not need.

Women always seemed to have more feelings for him than he did for them and the word *love* would often come up, which had Karim ending the relationship often before it started. He could never understand what it was with women and love. This "love" did not exist. It was nothing more than an infatuation. Women always confused hormones with emotions, he thought.

No doubt, Kim was one of these people. Western women were the worst when it came to this "love" thing. They were always looking for their so-called Prince Charming and he had no interest in being *that* man.

Karim sighed and returned to his work. It was not going to do itself. He wanted to make a good impression on their shareholders and in order to do so; he needed to understand his father's ledger. Something he could do without Kim's help. He just had to convert the documents over to modern spreadsheets.

Brought up by a father who ruled with an iron fist, Karim was taught that the only way to get things done was to do it yourself and to depend on a woman for assistance was tantamount to disaster. Their mother had died when Amare was only a few months old and the brothers were raised by a man who blamed their mother for dying and leaving them.

Unable to accept the loss of his wife to cancer, Saeed Sharqi raised his sons not to depend on women because they would only leave you in the end. Love, like all other emotions, was for those who didn't have businesses to run and money to make.

At twenty-five, Karim had embraced many of his father's traditional ways, but as he stared at his archaic accounting sheets, not for the first time did he question some of his father's beliefs.

Looking at the notes Kim had made, he knew that it would go much faster with her help, but he was certain that if he asked for it now, she would make him beg out of some sort of need for self-satisfaction. While he still didn't understand her motives, he knew that they couldn't be altruistic.

Chapter Eight

It was late afternoon and Kim and Amare had finished early for the day. He had been worried about his English exam and since he did so well, Kim decided to give him the rest of the day off and he had left to hang out with his friends.

After watching Zara pointedly ignore her, she decided that she wanted to get out of the house. Slipping into a sundress and her flats, she grabbed her hat and her books and went downstairs to find the driver to take her over to the orphanage. Unfortunately, he had decided to remain near Amare and would not be back for several hours. Sighing, Kim contemplated walking, but determined that it was much too hot to attempt that distance in this weather.

Hearing an engine, she looked up to see Karim driving around the corner toward the driveway. Waving to him, she realized that he was intentionally ignoring her, so she stepped in front of his car, forcing him to stop. Pasting a smile on her face, she ran around to the passenger side of his roadster, opened the door and jumped in.

Karim stared at her, opening and closing his mouth as he clutched at the steering wheel.

"What? Should I have knocked before opening this door too?" she asked cheekily as she waited for him to speak.

"Exactly, what do you think you are doing?" he finally asked her.

Reaching for the seatbelt, she fastened it around her, "The driver is out with Amare and I need a ride to the orphanage," she answered him.

"I am not going that way."

"The orphanage is on the way to every major road. You *are* going that way," she answered emphatically.

"No. I turn *before* the orphanage."

"Oh please, it's less than ten miles. If it's that much of an inconvenience, I would be happy to reimburse you for your gas," she offered.

"You will not," he told her through clenched teeth. Throwing the car into gear, he exited the driveway and headed toward the orphanage.

"Could we have some music?" she asked him, as she reached over to turn on the radio. Sitting back, she listened quietly to the traditional strains of Arabic music that must be coming from a CD. While Kim could appreciate different styles of music, she found the lack of any type of particular rhythm coupled with the harsh sounds from the violins too much for her frazzled nerves and she popped the CD out and tuned into a modern radio station. "Sorry, it's a bit too grating for me today," she told him as she settled back and began to tap her foot to the pop song.

"And this isn't?" he demanded.

Shrugging her shoulders, "Maybe but not in the same way. While I like some of the more modern artists, I find that the traditional music lacks any sort of comprehensive beat."

Squeezing the steering wheel as he drove, "It has been around considerably longer than this pop music," he replied as he sped up. The sooner he dropped her off and got away from her, the better.

"Don't get me wrong, I like many of the traditional beliefs that still exist in Saudi Arabia, but I've had a rough week and I'm not interested in listening to cats yowling as they scratch their nails across a chalkboard."

Slowing down, Karim took the next turn a bit too fast as Kim grabbed onto the door to hold on. Looking toward her, he realised that she was wearing a sundress and he could see her pale mounds poking out the top of her dress as they heaved up and down as she breathed.

Momentarily distracted, he looked back up as Kim cried out, "Look out!" Swerving, he narrowly avoided the oversized truck as the car left the asphalt and briefly rolled onto the hard packed sand.

He swore when he heard a loud noise that sounded much like a gunshot and quickly stopped the car. Looking at Kim, "Are you all right?" Unable to answer, Kim nodded her head before he got out of the car to check the damage. Walking around the car, he found the blown tire and kicked at it angrily. Moving to the back of the car, he opened the trunk and moved the contents out of the way to get to the spare tire.

Dropping the tire on the ground, he unhooked the jack and brought it around. Bending down, he placed the jack under the car and began to lift the car. He didn't realise that Kim had exited the car until he saw her bare legs come stand beside him.

Looking up, she had pulled her hat tightly down on her head as she watched him work. Before he could finish, there was another loud noise as the jack released and the car came crashing back down.

Slapping her hand over her mouth, Kim coughed as she masked her laugh.

"This is *not* funny," he told her as he replaced the jack and began again.

"Of course not," she told him as she snorted in amusement.

Suddenly the wind picked up and Kim's dress lifted showing off her legs as she squealed and pulled her dress tightly against her. Looking up, Karim wasn't sure which was more enticing, the view he got of her thighs or how tightly she currently had the dress moulded against her body. Turning back to the task at hand, he finished jacking up the car and reached for the wrench. As he was about to loosen them, Kim interrupted him.

"Um, aren't you supposed to loosen the lug nuts before you jack the car?" she asked him.

"Must you question *everything* I do?" he demanded as he slipped the wrench on a lug nut and went to loosen it. As he tried to loosen the nut, the tire turned causing him almost to lose his balance. Swearing loudly, he realised that he had forgotten to do just that at the same time she knew that she was right. Her laughter was better than any music as she began to laugh.

"Okay, while before, that was a little funny. This…this is a lot funny," she told him as she continued to laugh.

Closing his eyes, he got to a count of five before he realised that the wind had shifted. Standing up, he looked at the sky.

"We have to find shelter," he told her as he scanned the horizon for a safe place for them to seek refuge. "There's a storm coming."

"That's impossible," she told him. "I would have gotten a storm alert on my phone," she added as she pulled her phone out. Holding it up, "See, no alert."

Resisting the urge to throw the offending phone at the nearest rock, he tried for patience. "Look at the sky," he started as he pointed to the darkening clouds. "The wind that was just blowing, it has disappeared. We need to find shelter and we need to find it now."

Seeing that he was serious, Kim quickly pulled up a map of the area and found a shelter station less than a quarter mile from their location. Pointing it out to him, he went to the car to pull out his bag before grabbing her hand.

"Come on," he told her as he began to run across the sand. Moving as quickly as they could, they arrived at the shelter station as the sandstorm hit. Rushing inside, he slammed the door behind them as Kim turned on the flashlight on her phone. Grabbing it from her, he shined it around the room and chose a location far from the door and any windows. Taking her by the elbow, he escorted her over as she sat down on a bench.

Still using her flashlight, he searched the building for supplies but saw that it was empty. Hoping that the storm wouldn't last too long, he sat down in a huff and handed her back her phone. Seeing a smirk on her face, he tried to ignore it, but couldn't.

"What is it," he asked resignedly.

"Oh, nothing," she answered before giggling.

"Clearly that isn't the case."

Laughing, "I'm marvelling at how well we were able to meld traditional," she said as she motioned to the building they were in, "With modern," she finished as she waved her phone at him.

Scoffing, "If it wasn't for this *traditional* structure, we might not survive the storm," he told her as he crossed his arms.

"And if it wasn't for my phone, we wouldn't have known *about this traditional structure,*" she told him as she gloated.

"You know, we wouldn't even be here if you hadn't jumped in my car," he told her.

"No, we *might* not," she shot back. "You, on the other hand, might well be stuck on the road somewhere with no idea where to find shelter."

"I could have stayed in the car," he told her realising that he sounded as though he was sulking.

"As if that was any safer. Your tiny little sports car would be battered around like a balloon."

"I would have been fine."

"No, you would not."

"Why must you disagree with everything I say?" he demanded as he surged to his feet.

"Why must you act like a Neanderthal?" she shot back as she jumped up.

Grabbing her by the shoulders, he yanked her roughly toward him as she slammed against his chest. He stifled a groan when he felt her breasts swell against him. Gripping her chin between his thumb and forefinger, he tilted her head up toward him and stared down at her.

Kim's mouth was open as she gasped for breath. Biting her lower lip, she stared back at him, refusing to back down. She watched as his gaze shifted and he focused on her lower lip. With his finger, he rubbed back and forth along it causing tingles to spark throughout her body as she felt her knees begin to give. Sliding one arm around her waist, he easily held her against him as he continued to rub her lip.

Dipping his head down, he captured her lower lip between his and worried at it as she made small noises. Swiping his tongue between her lips, he easily delved inside sampling what she had to offer as she collapsed against him. Holding her tightly to him, he continued to kiss her as her hands found their way around his neck and tangled in his hair.

He tasted as good as she imagined, she thought to herself as she tentatively twined her tongue with his and smiled at his answering groan.

Reaching for the hem on her dress, he rubbed his hand up the outside of her leg before sliding around to cup her ass cheeks, kneading them as she began to make mewling noises of encouragement into his mouth.

As he was about to pull her dress over her head, he heard the sound of car doors slamming and his name being called. Breaking the kiss, he stepped back as Kim lost her balance and collapsed back onto the bench behind her.

Staring up at him in surprise, it took her a moment before she heard the voices calling Karim's name.

Within moments, Amare and the driver walked through the door, both looking relieved to see him. Turning his head, Amare was surprised to see Kim with his brother and she appeared to be upset.

"What is going on?" he asked them looking from one to the other.

Shrugging his shoulders, "No doubt you saw my car?" Karim asked. At Amare's nod, he continued. "I was driving Miss Atkins to the orphanage when the flat occurred. It looked as though a storm was coming, so we took shelter."

Turning his head, Amare waited for Kim to confirm the story as she nodded her head in response. Smiling, he turned back to his brother, "Is that all that was going on?"

"What do you mean?" Karim asked.

"Well, the storm never came, so I'm wondering what you might have been doing not to realise that," he said with a grin on his face.

"Nothing. At. All." Karim replied as Kim looked away. She didn't want to be involved in this conversation because they were very much doing something and she was disappointed that it had been interrupted.

Chapter Nine

It had been a week since the incident at the storm shelter and Kim sat on her bed stuffing her face with a sandwich that she had made for herself. Since they returned to the house, Karim had gone out of his way to avoid her and she couldn't stop thinking about him.

She wanted to kick herself. He was Amare's older brother. Nothing good could come from having feelings for him. She was not even certain if she had *any* feelings for him. Yes, she found him very attractive and when he kissed her, he had set her insides on fire in a way that no other man had ever done so, but it may well have been the heat of the moment.

Clearly, from the way he spoke to his brother, he didn't feel the same way and deep down, Kim knew that was for the best, but it didn't stop her from thinking about him. If he truly didn't feel anything, then why did he kiss her in the first place?

While she knew that she wasn't the most experienced person out there, she knew the sounds of pleasure when she heard it and he was certainly making them. If Amare hadn't arrived when he did, how far would he have taken it, she wondered.

She replayed in her head the warnings both Amare and Taleb gave her about Karim's avoidance of all things associated with relationships and love. While she knew that there had to be a reason for it, the brothers were convinced that it was simply part of who he was.

Suddenly Kim's Skype rang. She looked at her laptop screen to see who was calling and saw the profile picture of her best friend, Claire, pop up. Friends since they were children, the women Skyped almost every day since Kim came to Saudi Arabia to teach

"Claire!" Kim cried out as she answered the call.

"Kim!" Claire shouted back as they both laughed.

"It feels as if I haven't spoken to you in ages."

"It does feel like that doesn't it?"

"Yeah." Kim pouted before she stuffed the last of the sandwich in her mouth.

"I have some news!" Claire said with a big smile on her face. It was obvious that she was excited about something. Kim immediately leaned into her webcam.

"What is it?" she asked.

"I got accepted into Harvard Law School's library!" she shouted, waving a letter around. Kim jerked up and screamed.

"Oh, my God!"

"I know."

Both Kim and Claire screamed and laughed. They both knew how much Claire had wanted to work there and she was so proud of her best friend. She knew how hard she worked; she truly deserved to work at one of the top universities in the world. With her chestnut brown hair, heart-shaped face and piercing brown eyes, Claire was another example of beauty and brains.

"I am so proud of you, girl," Kim said to her as she hugged the laptop.

"What are you doing?" Claire burst into laughter.

"I have to embrace the laptop since I cannot hug you."

"Air hug then?"

"Exactly." Kim giggled. "Oh, you know what?"

"What is it?"

"Amare's older brother, Taleb, is starting at Harvard as well."

Claire raised her nicely shaped eyebrows. "Is he good looking?" she asked. Kim burst into laughter.

"Is that the first thing you are going to ask?"

"Why not?"

Kim shook her head. "Yes, he is. They all are." *Especially Karim,* she thought to herself.

"Are they now?" Claire looked and sounded interested. "Tell me about them."

"There is nothing much to tell."

"Liar."

Kim laughed. "Well, Amare is only sixteen." Before she finished speaking, Claire cut her off.

"Then let's not speak about the baby. On to the next," she said rubbing her hands together.

"Then there is Karim and Taleb."

"Which one is Karim?"

"The eldest son. He's *such* an asshole though."

"Is he?" Claire asked. Kim nodded. "It isn't surprising. You would expect that from rich people. I bet he is a player."

"I heard that he is. He does not date women for very long and I've been told that he doesn't believe in love."

Claire raised her eyebrows. "I am going to search for him on Google."

Kim laughed. Of course, Claire would do that. She was a curious one but so was Kim. She too had searched for the Sharqi family online. Moments later, Claire gasped.

"Well, this Karim dude is quite handsome," she said.

"He is average, I guess." Kim said. She did not want her confused feelings for him to show. So, she tried to down play it but she could not fool Claire. She knew her too well.

"Kimberley Atkins, this man is not average! And you do not think he is average, I can tell," Claire said narrowing her eyes. Kim laughed guiltily.

"Okay, he is not average." He was the most handsome man she had ever seen. He was just the right height and had a body that you wanted to reach out and touch.

"Exactly, you know he is very hot and you drool over him."

"Okay Claire, no one is drooling here."

"Wet dreams even."

"What?!" Kim started laughing. "You are ridiculous."

Claire giggled. "I bet you do." She winked. Kim shook her head as she briefly wondered if daydreams counted if she was awake.

"So what are you up to?" Kim asked, changing the subject. There had been too much of Karim in her life especially since he appeared to be purposely avoiding her. At the orphanage, that was all the other teachers could talk about and then, there was that moment in the storm shelter. Now Claire was talking about him.

"I am going out tonight to celebrate," Claire said. "What are you doing?"

"Hiding in my room."

"Wait. What? Why?"

Shrugging her shoulders, "Things got a bit awkward about a week ago."

Sliding closer to her webcam, "Oh? Spill it."

Sighing, Kim replied, "I kissed Karim. Or rather he kissed me. Oh, we kissed each other." She cringed at the squeals of laughter coming from Claire.

Just as Claire was about to respond, her phone beeped. Checking the message, she looked at her best friend apologetically, "Dammit, you should have lead with this, Kim, because I have to go. I'm going to be late, but we will be talking about this again," she told her ominously before laughing.

"Alright, bye love."

"Bye."

Kim signed off and put her laptop back on the nightstand wondering if she should have said anything to her friend. She still didn't know what the kiss meant. She lay on her bed facing the ceiling wondering what to do with herself. She had already planned her lessons.

Kim contemplated going downstairs to watch television but worried that she might run into Karim. Moments later, she heard the sound of a car engine. She got off her bed and went to the window to see whom it was.

She watched as a gorgeous woman in a tight fitting blue dress and black heels got out. Her long curly black hair cascaded down her back in waves. Middle Eastern women were very beautiful. Kim's jaw dropped when Karim got out of the car as well.

He was dressed in a fine black suit and he looked handsome as always. He said something to her, kissed her on the cheek and walked into the house while she waited outside. Kim could not help but feel a little jealous. It seemed as though he was going on a date with her.

Karim re-emerged moments later, they both got back into the car and Kim watched them drive off. A plain Jane like herself could never be with a guy like him. It was best for her to rein her emotions in and get a hold of herself. She sighed and walked away from the window. She sat on her bed, still confused about what to do. She was not tutoring Amare that day, so she had plenty of time on her hands.

Chapter Ten

Karim returned home late after a long date with Zainab. She was Sheikh Mufasa's eldest daughter and one of Sharqi Jewels biggest clients. Since taking over for his father as CEO, Karim had been working hard to build their client base since his father pulled that ridiculous stunt with a member of the royal family.

If it hadn't been for Taleb's quick thinking and the Tazeems desire not to cause further anguish for the family, they might well have lost everything. Since becoming CEO, Karim worked to blend many of his father's traditional ways with more modern expectations and so far, he had been successful. He hoped that by taking Zainab out and making sure that she was happy with him; her father would be as well. It was good business really.

As tired as he was, he still had work to do. When he walked into his office, he was surprised to find Kim sleeping at his desk with mounds of paper surrounding her.

He wondered what she was even doing in his office as he approached her. "Kim," he called out but she did not respond. She was fast asleep.

"Kim, wake up," he said but she was not budging. Grunting, he took off his suit jacket and slung it over a chair. Walking back around his desk, he put one arm under Kim's thighs and the other around her waist.

Lifting her easily, he was surprised at how light she was as he settled her in his arms. He froze when her head rolled against his chest and she sighed. Her hair brushed against his chin as he inhaled deeply noting that she smelled of vanilla and some sort of flower. Shaking his head, he strode out of the room and easily mounted the steps.

Moments later, he walked into her bedroom and gently placed her on the bed. He could not believe how heavy a sleeper she was that she did not wake during all that. He smiled as he looked at her, her hair was a tumbled mass around her head and her long lashes stood out against her pale skin, which was dotted with freckles.

***

Kim opened her eyes to find Karim standing above her, staring down at her. She could not figure out if she was awake or asleep. She had been dreaming about him, only in her dream they had been riding in his car and he had stopped to kiss her.

But then, the last thing she remembered was being in his office sorting out his figures. When and how would she have gotten into her bed? And why would Karim be there in her room? The only answer she had was that she was still dreaming. There was only one way to find out.

Kim sat up and placed her hand on Karim's rock hard abs. He stood there, frozen in place, looking at her. She was now convinced that she was dreaming. If she was awake and touching him like that, he would probably dismiss her as he always did.

So, Kim decided to run her hand along his abs and up his chest. Karim grunted as he felt her touching him. He dipped his head lower and pressed his lips firmly against hers. Kim welcomed his lips gladly and responded when he kissed her, eagerly kissing him back. It was a fast, passionate and hungry kiss.

The kiss was too real as Kim's entire body tingled in response to his touch on her lips. Her feet curled reflexively as she felt pleasure tendrils unfurl throughout her body. She felt like she was on fire as every fibre of her being was responding to this man, which was when she realised that she was not asleep.

There was no way the kiss could feel this good in a dream. She wanted to scream out but it was too late. She was already kissing him and she was enjoying it too much to stop.

Karim broke off the kiss and stared into Kim's piercing blue eyes. Their chests rose up and down as they struggled to restore the breath they had lost. No one moved, they simply stared at each other. The only sound that filled the room was the sound of their heavy breathing. Karim's dark gaze made Kim feel even more aroused as her eyes darkened in response. His jaw twitched.

Leaning down, Karim grabbed the hem of her t-shirt and lifted it over her head, tossing it aside. Looking down at her admiringly, he watched as her blush spread down her neck to the tops of her breasts. Unable to resist, he cupped her breasts, holding them in his hands as he kneaded them under his sure fingers. His thumbs brushed across her nipples as they hardened to stiff peaks.

Pushing her legs apart, he dropped to his knees between them, now eye level with her. His hands never left her breasts as he watched the play of emotions across her face as she became more aroused at his light touch. Leaning forward, he swiped his tongue out to lick one nipple as she gasped. He chuckled against her breast when she grabbed his head, pushing it against her chest eager for more.

Alternating back and forth, he pulled and twisted lightly at one nipple while he happily sucked and licked the other one, applying pressure and enjoying how responsive she was to him.

Lifting his head, Kim was shocked to see the intensity of his arousal on his face as she moaned in response. Unused to men being turned on by her, she was surprised at how arousing his desire was for her.

Sliding his hands down the sides of her body, he wrapped his hands around her hips and pulled her closer to the edge of the bed. Digging his fingers into her ass cheeks, his fingertips brushed along her now very moist centre, which made her squirm in response.

Capturing her lips again, he greedily plundered her mouth surprised that she now matched his actions, dancing and twisting her tongue around his until they were both breathless. Melting against him, Karim broke the kiss as she tilted her head to the side. Taking it as an open invitation, he nuzzled against the nape of her neck, pressing kisses against her more sensitive spots as she moaned in response.

Once again, mimicking him, she kissed along his neck, sucking lightly at his earlobe as he hissed in response. Tilting her head up, she dipped her tongue in his ear as he stilled. The low growl from the back of his throat was enough to tell her that she was doing it right as he began to stroke his fingers up and down her back.

Wanting to touch him as much as he was touching her, she reached for the buttons on his shirt and began fumbling to release them. Grumbling at her lack of coordination, she couldn't pull the buttons loose fast enough. Stilling her hands, he leaned back and quickly unbuttoned his shirt.

Slipping it off, he tossed it on the nearest chair. As he turned back toward her, she stopped him.

Touching his face, she smiled shyly, still half wondering if this was all some sort of an elaborate dream and if it was, she didn't want it to end. Tracing her finger along his lips, she yelped and then giggled when he nipped at her finger. Pulling her hand away, she was surprised when he stopped her.

Holding her hand in his, he kissed the palm of her hand as she caught her breath.

How could something so innocent set her insides on fire, she wondered as he then nipped at her fingers. Sucking hard at each one until her eyes fluttered closed and she moaned.

"Karim," she moaned as she ran her hands over his chest, which felt as though it had been chiselled from marble. Everything about him was perfection, she thought, as she stroked his smooth skin and watched in fascination as the muscle rippled beneath her touch.

"Do you want me as much as I want you?" Karim whispered against her ear before he nibbled on it.

"I do." Kim moaned.

"I haven't been able to get you out of my mind since that day in the storm shelter."

"Hmmm…me too."

Kim could barely concentrate on what he was saying. His whisper betrayed how turned on he was by her and she dared not speak certain that she wouldn't make any sense. She was caught off guard when he pushed her onto her back.

Reaching for the waistband on her shorts, he grabbed them along with her panties. Lifting her leg, she pressed her foot against his shoulder and lifted her hips as he pulled them both off and tossed them to the floor.

He grabbed her ankle before she could put her foot down and kissed her instep before slowly kissing his way up her leg. When he got near her apex, he switched to the other leg, his feather light kisses making her pant as she flexed her feet in response.

Rubbing his hands up and down the insides of her thighs, he slid his hands over to her hips and lifted her toward him. Stroking up and down her fold, he was surprised at how wet she was and could no longer resist her heady scent as he dipped his head down and licked up her slit. Her tiny little clit was as stiff as a pearl as he bathed it with his tongue.

Unprepared for her response, he tightened his grip on her hips as she bowed up, crying out his name as her body thrashed beneath him. Holding her tightly to him, he pressed his tongue inside and licked at her pleasure as she continued to thrash beneath him with each swipe of the tongue.

As her orgasm subsided, Kim felt as though her spine had melted as she lay sprawled on the mattress. She barely registered when she felt him move away from her until she felt a light breeze along her fevered skin.

Leaning up on her elbows, she watched as he released the clasp on his trousers and drew the zipper down. Kicking off his shoes and removing his socks, he stepped out of his trousers and stood there in his briefs, the painful evidence of his arousal, straining against the fabric.

Reaching for the waistband, he drew them down, allowing his impressive member to spring free. Rolling to her side, Kim stared, fascinated, at the pre-cum that glistened on his head.

Crooking her finger at him in a come hither motion, he stepped toward her as she reached her hand out, enjoying the texture of his tight smooth skin as she ran her fingers up and down his erection. Her thumb brushed against the pre-cum and she brought it to her mouth, licking her thumb clean as he groaned in response.

Unable to wait any longer, he reached down and scooped her up, tossing her farther up the bed as he joined her. Leaning over her, he rested his weight on his arms as he looked down at her. Her long hair was splayed across the pillow and her blue eyes had grown dark with arousal.

Nestling himself between her legs, he rocked his hips, pushing her legs farther apart. Reaching down between them to make sure that she was ready, he closed his eyes when he felt how wet she was. Positioning himself, he slowly pushed his way in, concerned that he might hurt her.

At the pace he was going, Kim thought that she might scream in frustration as she lifted her hips impatiently. Wrapping her legs around him, she met his thrust with one of her own, catching him by surprise as he ended up buried deeply inside her.

They both groaned in satisfaction as he began to thrust in and out. Each downward thrust was met by the quivering of her vaginal muscles, which clutched eagerly at his invading member.

Karim wanted to go slow, but as her need arose, she began to shake beneath him, making it difficult for him to keep going as his thrusts became more chaotic. Thrusting faster, he felt her pleasure spill over as she cried out his name, clutching tightly to his shoulders. With a low moan, he couldn't hold out any longer as his own orgasm rolled through and he shortened his thrusts, as he emptied his seed deep inside her.

Collapsing, he rolled to the side, taking her with him, reluctant to let her go yet as his erection slowly dropped down. Hugging her to him, he kissed her eyelids as she stifled a yawn.

Stroking her back, he felt her breathing even out and within moments, she was asleep again. Smiling down at her, he kissed the top of her head and held her in his arms while he drifted off to sleep.

Chapter Eleven

Kim awoke to find a naked Adonis in her bed. Her eyes flew open when she realised that it was Karim. She blushed as memories of their night of passion flooded her mind. Was she really that bold?

When she had awakened to see him standing over her, she was sure that she had been dreaming and when he didn't stop her, the urge to fulfil her fantasies took over. This was not normal behaviour for her. She would never come onto a man first.

Now Karim was going to think that she was that kind of woman. Well, she wasn't solely to blame. He let her touch him, and then kissed her. And that kiss had felt so magical. Kim glanced over when she felt Karim begin to stir as she saw him slowly waking up. Still too shy to face him after last night, she instantly closed her eyes to act as if she was still sleeping.

The aftermath of their actions worried her. Amare had already warned her about his attitude with women. For her, this was the best night of her life. For him, it was probably just another one-night stand.

He would probably go about his business as if nothing had happened. Karim grunted as he sat up. Keeping her eyes tightly closed, she felt him get out of bed and could hear the rustle of clothes, as he got dressed.

"I am returning to my room to shower," he told her flatly, as she opened her eyes in surprise. Not even a good morning, she thought to herself as she watched him get dressed.

To her surprise, he leaned down to kiss her cheek as he grinned at her, "Did you think that I didn't know you were pretending to sleep?" he asked her before standing back up. "I'll see you at breakfast."

Shaking her head, Kim climbed out of bed and walked to the shower. *How could he be so casual about last night*, she asked herself. Maybe it was best to put last night's events behind her. Karim was Amare's older brother and it wouldn't be appropriate to have a relationship with him while she was tutoring his younger brother. No matter how hard it was, she was not going to develop feelings for him.

After a long shower, Kim got dressed and made her way downstairs for breakfast. She was very hungry. As she walked toward the dining room, she noticed the maids looking at her a little more than usual. Some were even whispering amongst themselves. Kim thought it odd but she decided to shrug it off. Moments later, she walked into the dining room to find Karim already seated at the table dressed in a charcoal grey shirt and grey trousers. He looked and smelled good. He was looking over some paper work as usual.

Joining him at the table, Kim served herself some food and immediately started eating. Karim looked up, "Did you go in my office to work on the accounts?" he asked her.

"Yes," she replied. Not only had she been bored, but she was worried about the outdated accounts. Clearly, he needed help with them even if he was too proud to ask for her assistance. They had been created using old formulas and old digital systems that from the looks of his notes, he was lost.

"How much did you do?"

"I basically got through most of it."

Karim raised his eyebrows. "Explain to me what you did," he said to her. Kim moved closer to him and started explaining and pointing out what she had done. He listened as she spoke, asking questions and having her go over some areas again.

"The formulas are all set up. So I would recommend inputting all the data into Excel as it will make it much easier to keep track of instead of this method," she said as Karim frowned.

"I will think about it," he replied. Kim stared at him blankly.

Pursing her lips, she shook her head, why was he always disagreeing with her?

"Given the amount of data, it would be of the greatest benefit to your company to update your accounting to something, oh at least from the twentieth century," she told him dryly. "That way you can, as a minimum, provide your shareholders with something logical instead of…this," she finished gesturing to the handwritten ledgers.

As Karim was about to respond, two maids walked into the room, one was carrying a tray of fruit. They glanced over at Karim and then at Kim before they placed the tray on the table. There was something strange going on; Kim thought to herself. Why were they looking at her like that?

"Sheik Karim, is there anything else we could get you?" one of them maids asked him.

"No, you may go." He dismissed them with his hand as they bowed their heads and left the room.

"What if I wanted something?" Kim muttered under her breath. The maids had not even asked her or even looked at her when they asked Karim. This was ridiculous.

She glanced over to Karim. It was still hard for her to believe that they that had spent a night filled with passion and were now sitting together as strangers. Trying to put it behind her, she concentrated on her breakfast but was soon pushing her fork aimlessly around the plate as her mind wandered.

While she didn't have a tremendous amount of experience, he was a magnificent lover and she had lost track of the number of times she climaxed in such a short time. And while he could have easily taken what he wanted and left, he made sure that her own pleasure came first, which had never happened to her before.

She jumped when she heard him shuffling the papers. Looking up, she watched as he put them together and placed them in a folder. "Was this everything?" he asked her.

Nodding her head, "Other than the need to use *computerised* software, yes," she told him.

Karim had half a smile on his face. "Well, they were my father's files."

"And while some schools do still teach how to use an abacus, I think that you'll find the use of a computer to be a bit more sophisticated."

"I've heard you woman."

Kim smiled and decided to serve herself some more eggs. She was feeling particularly hungry that morning. Fortunately, the maids always served a lot of food.

"Are you enjoying yourself there?" Karim asked her.

"Huh?" she looked at him.

"You eat a lot." He looked at her with a blank facial expression.

"I seem to be unusually hungry this morning."

"Of course you are hungry. Moaning that much must have taken a lot of energy."

Kim's jaw dropped open. Was he really making fun of her? He was right though, she had moaned a lot the night before.

"I did *not* moan that much," she answered petulantly.

"Is that so?"

"Yes, I'm not a moaner." Kim gulped down some orange juice.

"We will see about that." Kim's eyes flew open when she felt his hand on her leg as he began caressing her inner thighs.

"What are you doing?" she breathed.

"Proving my point."

"Whaaaa-" she could not even finish her sentence without moaning. Karim stared into her eyes as she shifted in her seat. Damn, how was he able to turn her on so fast while they were sitting in the dining room?

"See what I mean?"

"Shut up," she mumbled as his fingers brushed lightly across her panties. All of a sudden, he stopped touching her as Kim's eyes flew open. She watched as he picked up his files and rose from the table.

"Karim!" she complained as he smiled mischievously at her.

"I have proven my point."

"What? Where are you off to?" Kim asked as she tried to even out her breathing. How could he just touch her like that and then stop abruptly? Didn't he feel anything? Shaking her head, she willed her body to calm down as she watched him.

"I have a meeting to attend," he said right before he walked out of the dining room. Kim gulped down more juice. She needed to cool down after that mini session. She leaned back in the chair and started fanning herself.

Fortunately, none of the maids had walked into the room as that would have been embarrassing.

No longer hungry, she pushed her plate aside. Was all this simply a game to him? Shaking her head, she turned in her chair and got unsteadily to her feet. She simply had to put him out of her mind, but how?

Chapter Twelve

"Good morning, Sheik," the receptionist greeted Karim with a big smile on her face as he walked into Sharqi Jewels Head Office.

"Morning," he said to her as he kept walking and barely paid attention to her blushing over him.

"Sheik Hussain Tazeem is waiting for you in your office," she said.

"Thank you." Karim nodded.

While Hussain was eight years older than he was, they had grown up near one another and were both the product of traditional upbringings. Both hard workers, Karim had come to rely on him as both an ally and a friend.

He had been shocked when he found out about his father's behaviour toward Hussain's twin sister and quickly sought to make amends. He walked into his office to find Hussain sitting comfortably at his desk.

"Hussain," Karim said as he walked in. Hussain got up and went to greet him.

"Karim. It has been a while, my friend," he said with a huge smile on his face.

"It has indeed." The two of them shook hands and sat back down. Hussain pressed a button on the phone. "Bring us some tea," he said and let go of the button. He returned his attention back to his friend as he smiled at him.

"How has business been going?" Hussain asked him.

"Sharqi Jewels is progressing well. After his forced retirement, my father wasn't particularly cooperative explaining some of the files, so there has been considerable work figuring out exactly what is going on financially."

"I can only imagine."

The receptionist walked into the office with a tray of tea, which she placed on the desk. Karim took a sip of his black tea before he spoke.

"There is much to do but we are no strangers to hard work," he said.

"Yes, indeed," Hussain replied as he laughed.

Both men were from powerful families. The Tazeems had their hands in oil and spices while the Sharqis had their hands in jewels. As the eldest sons, both men put the growth and prosperity of the family business before their own personal lives. They were very similar in many ways, which was why they were so close.

"How is the spices industry these days?" Karim asked.

"Good." Hussain nodded and drank some of his tea.

"And the business with my father?"

"That is all well too."

Karim shook his head. "My father is a particular man," he said. A few months ago, Karim's father had reluctantly gone into business with Hussain and to his surprise, it had become quite profitable.

"That may be the case; however he is a good business man."

"His ways are so outdated; I was trying to decipher his old business accounts the last few weeks."

Hussain started laughing. "And how is that going?" he asked.

"Not very easy, I tell you."

Talking about those business accounts reminded Karim of Kim. He was surprised that she had taken it upon herself to help him out with them. Even though he did not want to admit it, he was grateful. She had helped him a great deal and saved him a lot of time.

She had surprised him when she came onto him the night before. He had never thought she was the forward type. If he did not need to be at the office early that morning, he would have made love to her again.

The short time they had spent together over breakfast had been distracting as he found her sweet scent intoxicating. He would have loved to continue with the teasing and watch as he brought her pleasure. The small noises that she made as she writhed beneath him were arousing and he couldn't wait to do it again.

"As long as it is working out," Hussain said with a smile. "So listen, I have a favour to ask of you."

Karim blinked a few times. "Yes, anything," he said. This was not the time Karim had been caught thinking about Kim.

"You remember Cassie?" Hussain asked him.

"Your Western woman?" Karim asked as he looked at Hussain with a narrowed gaze.

"Yes, her." Hussain smiled and shook his head.

"What about her?" Karim asked. The couple of times that he had met her, he found her too American for his taste.

"When she was younger, she used to walk past this jewellery shop every day. She fell in love with a particular ring."

"Okay?" Karim furrowed his brow. He wondered where Hussain was going with this.

"Well, I need your help in locating that ring," Hussain said. Karim raised his eyebrows and put his cup on the desk.

"What? You are not thinking of marrying this woman are you?" he asked. He went from being confused to being shocked. He stared at Hussain with his eyes widened and waited for an explanation. He was really hoping that Hussain was not going to propose.

"You look surprised," Hussain replied.

"I am surprised. What happened to the man who did not believe in marriage?"

That was another thing that Karim and Hussain had in common. They both did not believe in love and they did not want to get married either. They never wanted to be tied down to anyone, especially a mere woman.

Hussain sighed before he responded. "That man met Cassie."

"Even after you found out that she was a spy?" Karim questioned.

"Well she did not sabotage me in the end. She actually helped me."

"It does not change her initial intentions. This is why women cannot be trusted."

Hussain laughed loudly. "That was how I used to think; however things are different now. I found someone worth trusting and loving." Karim leaned back in his leather chair and stared at his friend.

"So, you want me to locate some kind of ring, so that you can marry a spy?" Karim had been aware of how Cassie and Hussain had met. He had been surprised that Hussain stayed with her, even after he knew that she was an industrial spy. Even though she had changed her ways, Karim would have never been able to trust her after finding out her original intentions.

Hussain narrowed his gaze at Karim and leaned forward. "I need you find that ring for me so that I can marry the woman I love."

"Who happens to be a spy."

"Who *used* to be a spy."

The two men started laughing.

"Okay. What kind of a ring is it?" Karim asked.

"It was a unique gold band with a red stone. Around the stone were yellow diamonds," Hussain explained. "I will have a mock up drawn."

"It sounds like a unique ring," Karim said, scratching his stubble with his thumb.

"I purchased the entire store and I will have the contents shipped here. I just need Sharqi Jewels to locate the exact ring." Karim widened his eyes and stared at Hussain as if he had lost his mind. He was starting to think that he might have actually lost it.

"You did what?" Maybe Karim had heard wrong. "You bought the entire shop?"

"Yes, and the warehouse."

Karim shook his head. "My friend, you are crazy." Hussain laughed.

"Crazy in love," he replied as Karim ran his hand through his wavy hair.

"All of this for one girl?" Karim asked, whistling lowly. It made no sense to him. Hussain was going to great lengths for one woman, a western woman at that. He really could not understand his friend.

"You'll understand one day, my friend." Hussain said to him with a warm smile on his face. Karim raised his eyebrows, shaking his head.

Chapter Thirteen

As Kim was walking out of her classroom at the orphanage, she heard excited voices coming from the teacher's lounge. Curious, she headed toward the lounge and was surprised to see Karim standing there surrounded by the teachers who were busy bombarding him with questions.

Instead of his usual look of indifference, he looked downright terrified as the women fawned over him. Amused, Kim stood in the doorway watching as he tried to answer their questions as fast as they asked them. When Dania began asking him about the number of children he planned to have, Kim took pity on him and cleared her throat as loud as she could.

Turning his head, the look of relief Karim gave her had her covering her mouth to mask her laugh as her eyes danced merrily. Shaking his arms, he stepped away from the doting women and rushed toward her.

"I thought we could go to lunch," he told her quickly, as she looked at him in surprise.

"Um, sure. Just let me grab my things," Kim replied, as she wondered what got into him.

"Oh, Kim, must he leave so soon?" Salma asked. "We were just getting to know him," she crooned as she batted her eyelashes at him.

Sliding her hands up his arm, Dania leaned against him, "Can't we keep him for just a little bit longer?" she asked as she winked at Kim.

Turning away, Kim coughed to cover her laugh again when she saw the horrified look on Karim's face. Turning back, "Perhaps another time, ladies, there was mention of lunch," she told them as the women made noises of complaint.

Stepping forward, Karim grasped her elbow and quickly exited the lounge as the women all shouted their goodbyes to him. Once outside, he took several deep breaths as he heard the women's laughter from inside.

"Is it always like that in there?" he asked as they walked toward the car.

Unable to hold her laughter back, "No, that was a special show just for you," she answered as she clutched at her sides.

When they arrived at the restaurant, Kim stepped out of the car and looked up. "Where are we?"

"This restaurant belongs to a friend of mine. Come on, I think that you will enjoy it."

Placing his hand at the small of her back, he escorted her inside. As they walked toward the reception stand, he was surprised to see Hussain. Smiling broadly at his friend, they shook hands as Karim introduced them to each other before Hussain showed them to a table overlooking the back garden.

Giving him a strange look, Hussain held his tongue as he handed them their menus.

Opening her menu, Kim looked at the broad list of options and sighed. "So what's good here?" she asked him as Karim closed his menu.

"Everything."

"Well, I'm not that hungry. Any chance you could be more specific?"

Smiling at her, "Is there anything that you're in the mood for?"

"Food," she replied as she snorted in amusement. "Actually, I've liked everything I've tried so far. Maybe we could order some different appetizers so that I can try them. Oh, and dessert."

"So, should we start with the dessert first?" he asked her flatly.

Looking up at him, Kim wasn't sure if he was serious until she saw his mouth twitch. Pasting a frown on her face, she stared at him, "I think I can manage the appetizers first," she told him. "Unless of course, the desserts are really good."

"Oh, they are. Hussain's twin sister is a fantastic pastry chef."

As she was about to say something, the waitress came to their table to take their order. Karim ordered a selection of finger foods and pastries for Kim to try.

They chatted together while they waited and Kim was surprised at how attentive he was. While he did interrupt their conversation to check his phone several times, he always seemed able to pick up the conversation where they left off, which impressed her. If she wasn't careful, she could easily see herself falling for this man despite the warnings she received from his brothers.

When their food arrived, Kim looked at the array of finger foods all sitting on small plates. Everything smelled delicious, as she took a deep breath, smiling.

"I noticed that you seem to enjoy the different pastries that our cook makes and thought that you might like to try some of our more savoury dishes."

Nodding her head, Kim couldn't prevent the blush from creeping into her cheeks as she realised that Karim watched her eat. Reaching for a meat tart, she bit into it and closed her eyes.

"Oh, that's delicious," she told him as she licked the juice off her lips. She paused when she saw that he was staring at her. Licking her lips again, she watched his eyes darken as he focussed on her mouth.

"So, which ones do you like?" she asked him trying to break the sudden tension.

Reaching across the table, he picked up what looked like a miniature pie and bit into it without breaking eye contact with her. Chewing slowly, Kim watched as he swallowed before he reached his hand across to her to give her the remaining bite.

Unsure what to do, she stared at his hand for what felt like several minutes as he patiently waited for her to open her mouth.

Finally opening her mouth, he placed the tart in her mouth as she bit down on it. Closing her eyes, she enjoyed the mix of spices as she chewed. "Oh, that's so good," she commented as he grinned at her.

The tension now broken, the couple enjoyed their lunch occasionally feeding each other morsels as if they had been doing so for years. Neither of them noticed Hussain watching them, pleased for his friend who had yet to realise that he too had fallen for an American woman. "Welcome to the club, my friend," he mumbled under his breath.

Chapter Fourteen

After lunch, they returned to the house, laughing and talking as if they were old friends. Walking inside, Kim was surprised to see that no one was home. Karim had excused himself to go take care of some messages, which left her on her own and unsure what to do.

As she walked upstairs, she caught sight of something reflecting outside. Walking to the window, she saw that it was a swimming pool and couldn't believe that she had never noticed it before. On a whim, she ran up to her room to put on her swimsuit.

Coming back downstairs, she exited out through the courtyard and walked toward the pool, which sparkled like turquoise in the sun. Dropping her towel and kicking off her shoes, she looked over her shoulder toward the house, but didn't see anyone.

With a whoop, she ran toward the pool and leaped up, curling into a ball as she went crashing in. Surfacing, she laughed aloud as she swam to the side. Resting her arms, she took in the opulent surroundings as tropical plants enclosed the pool making it look like an oasis in the desert.

Rolling to her back, she floated to the middle of the pool, closing her eyes against the bright light, as she enjoyed the sun's rays. A loud splash startled her as she sat up suddenly. Looking around, she didn't see anything but yelped when she felt a hand on her leg tugging her down.

Turning around in the water, she was surprised to see Karim staring back at her from under the water. Surfacing again, she laughed as he caught her around the waist.

"I thought you were in your office," she sputtered, suddenly feeling the heat from his body as he pulled her closer.

"I was, but then I heard yelling so thought that I would go investigate. Imagine my surprise when I saw you doing a cannon ball into the pool."

Laughing, "Sorry. If I had this incredible pool, I would be in it all the time," she told him as he tugged her toward the deep end. Holding onto his arm to steady herself, she allowed him to pull her.

"My mother loved to swim," Karim commented. "She was the one who insisted that we put it in. It rarely gets used anymore. I'm surprised that my father still keeps it maintained."

"Why wouldn't you want to use it? It's fantastic."

Smiling, Karim looked around seeing the pool from her perspective, "Yes, I guess it is. When my mother died, my father shut down. He blamed her for leaving us and everything that was good and beautiful was suddenly forbidden as he turned into the formidable man he is today."

"That's terrible. How did your mother die?"

"Cancer," he answered simply.

"I'm so sorry. You were so young."

"I was. Amare does not even remember her. I can tell when he looks at her picture that he sees a stranger." Shaking his head to clear the bad thoughts, he pushed her lightly away. "Enough sad talk," he told her as he splashed her.

Squealing, Kim splashed him back and they spent the next few minutes chasing each other around the pool. Jumping on him, she attempted to pull him under the water when he pushed her up against the wall. Breathing heavily, her laughter turned to pants as he pressed against her, their wet skin sticking to each other as one of Kim's fantasies suddenly became real.

Cupping the sides of her face, he kissed her gently as her body immediately took over demanding more. Tendrils of pleasure that he was so good at unfurling began to spread around her body as she pushed her feet flat against the wall to keep them from curling in response.

She was so wrapped up in the kiss that she didn't realise that he had pulled the tie on her swim top until she felt the breeze on her exposed breasts. Looking frantically around, she attempted to cover herself but he stopped her.

"Relax, no one can see you," he told her as he tugged at the tie on her bikini bottom. Pulling it loose, he tossed her swimsuit on the side of the pool before he pulled her unresisting body toward him.

His eyes darkened as he watched her floating toward him. Grabbing her legs, he helped her straddle him as she settled her hands on his shoulders. Turning so he was leaning against the wall, he kissed her again as she stroked her hands over his body.

Kim couldn't believe that she was out in the open and naked as her traitorous body greedily accepted everything he had to offer her. While that little voice in the back of her head warned her again about getting too close to him, she steadfastly ignored it, determined to enjoy this moment.

Lightly tracing her fingers down his body, she came up against an obstacle as her hand settled on his briefs. Breaking the kiss, she gave him a stern look.

"Someone appears to be overdressed," she commented as she fought the urge to giggle.

"Indeed. Perhaps you could help me out with that?"

Grinning at him, she climbed off his lap and pressed up against him, using her feet as support to keep from floating away. Taking a deep breath, she sunk under water and using her hands, pulled herself down. Sliding her fingers along his waistband, she tugged his briefs over his hips, not realising that it would be more difficult to do under water.

Finally succeeding, she pulled them down and off his feet. As she was about to surface, she brushed against his erection and it bounced playfully in front of her. Unable to resist, she wrapped her hand around it, before opening her mouth and drawing it in. Karim's sudden thrashing made her pause as she rose to the surface to toss his briefs next to her swimsuit.

Before she could ask him what's wrong, he wrapped his arms around her and pulled her tightly against him as he kissed her. All the past weeks' angst and turmoil melted away. Despite her need for caution, when she was in his arms, she felt as though she were home and there was no place else that she wanted to be.

Closing her eyes, she kissed him back as their tongues danced together twining back and forth. Placing his hands on the outside of her thighs, he lifted her so that she was straddling him again. His erection bounced against her stomach as she moaned into his mouth.

Reaching down, he rubbed his fingers along her slit and smiled when he felt that she was ready for him. Positioning himself, he slowly pressed into her as she rocked her hips to accommodate him.

Once he was seated, he held tight to her hips as he rocked her back and forth along his shaft. Placing her feet against the wall, she used it as leverage so that she could thrust harder against him.

As he continued to thrust into her, Kim held tight to his shoulders. Leaning in, she sucked on his lower lip as he growled in response and sped up.

Moaning, Kim rocked harder as his thrusts became more chaotic. Within moments, her orgasm rolled through her as she cried out into his mouth.

One, two, three more thrusts and Karim was coming, her spasms speeding him up as she milked him dry.

As they finished, Kim sagged against him as he kissed the top of her head.

The sound of a ringing phone caught their attention as he set her aside to answer it. Speaking animatedly into the phone, he exited the pool and grabbed his clothes, walking back to the house without saying a word to her.

Staring after him, Kim couldn't believe that he didn't say anything to her as she wondered if he would come back. Given that he had taken his clothes with him, she assumed that he wouldn't as she fumed.

Both Taleb's and Amare's warnings echoed in her head as her brain reminded her that he was not into relationships. Swearing, she got out of the pool and wrapped herself up in her towel before scooping up her swimsuit and stalking back to the house.

This would be the last time she allowed Karim Sharqi near her, she vowed.

Chapter Fifteen

A couple of weeks later, Karim finally decided to take Kim's advice and update the company's accounts. While he should have done it when Kim told him; Karim did things on his terms and would not be ordered around by a woman.

Since that one night they had spent together as well as the incident at the pool, it appeared as if Kim was going out of her way to avoid him, which was probably for the best as he still had much work to do. But that didn't stop him from thinking about her.

He still remembered how soft her skin had felt and how good she tasted. Every time he touched her, she had been so responsive to him. So much so that there were times that he could think of nothing else, but he had too much work to do.

Karim headed out of his home office and walked down the corridor. As he was walking, he spied Kim walking down the hall staring at her phone. She gasped when Karim stood right in front of her.

"You scared me," she told him, clutching her chest.

"I updated my software," he said with a smile.

Kim raised her eyebrows. "Well, it took you long enough." She shook her head.

"Meet me in your room, in five minutes," he said quietly to her. Kim raised her eyebrows in question. She looked at him and saw a dangerous and dark look. She had seen it in his eyes the night they had sex.

She should tell him no, she told herself, as her mouth answered, "Okay," cautiously. Kim felt her body heat up and her fingers tingle as she watched Karim walk off. She so badly wanted to follow him straightaway, but Amare and his friends had been complaining about their upcoming exam.

She had told him that she would drop by to answer their questions, so she headed to his study room where she found them sitting around the room with their laptops and books. Kim stepped into the air-conditioned room and approached them.

"Hi guys, I'm here. Let's get started!" It was only going to take a couple of minutes; she thought to herself. She might as well help them and then go meet Karim. He had not even said why he wanted her to meet him in her room anyway.

"Great!" Amare said to her. He looked so relieved to see her.

"So what do you guys need help with?"

"Here, take a look." Amare showed her a past exam paper. Kim read the questions and started working through the questions with Amare and his friends.

***

Karim paced the room impatiently while he waited for Kim to come to her room. He had told her to meet him in five minutes and it had been much longer than that. He lay on her bed completely naked, his thumbs drumming against his chest. He was growing more and more impatient by the minute.

He saw the door opening. Finally, she had come to him. He was definitely going to punish her with a few hard spanks for making him wait for so long. He told her five minutes and it had been at least thirty. No one made him wait, they would not dare. What had she been doing anyway?

"Father!" Karim shouted and quickly covered his manhood with one of Kim's pillows.

"Karim!" his father shouted and took a few steps back.

Karim got off the bed and quickly slipped on his trousers. What on earth was his father doing in Kim's bedroom?

"What are you doing here?" Karim asked his father.

"That is what I should be asking you. Why is it that you are laying on her bed, NAKED?" the sheik shouted at his son.

"That is my business, father. Why are you sneaking into her room?"

Karim was angry with his father. What right did he have to sneak into her room? It definitely warranted an explanation. Karim buckled his belt and placed his hands on his hips. He stared at his father and waited for an explanation; however, he did not receive one.

"So, you are sleeping with the American woman?" he asked. He shook his head in disappointment with his son.

"What does that have to do with you?"

"She is a westerner!"

"So what? I love her." Karim could not believe that those words had left his mouth. He hadn't even gotten the chance to admit it to himself and come to terms with it.

"You what? Don't make me laugh," Saeed Sharqi barked. "You are my eldest son! You must lead by example and be with a full Arabic woman."

"I can be with whomever I choose to be."

"Over my dead body," Saeed shouted. Karim was not surprised that his father did not approve of him being with a Westerner. He too never wanted a western woman but Kim was different. She was a smart and beautiful woman.

It was unlike him but he couldn't stop himself from developing feelings for her.

"Father, you need to stop being so controlling and outdated with everything. What harm will Kim bring?" Karim shouted. He never shouted at his father but at the moment, he was so angry, he could not control himself.

"She is not Arabic! Those westerners have no culture. You cannot bring me a foreigner as a daughter-in-law," Saeed said, pacing across the bedroom.

"All I said is that I love her." There were those words again. He said them without even thinking. "There is no ring, so relax father."

"Love? What do you know about love boy?"

"Probably more than you will ever know. You do not know how to love anyone, not even your children."

The sheik shook his head. "Being with her has already changed you. When have you ever spoken to me like that?" he demanded. "That spoilt American brat!"

Karim could not believe the things his father was saying about her. She was one of the most humble people that he knew. He picked up his shirt and walked out of the room leaving his father standing there by himself.

"Don't you dare walk away when I am still talking to you!" Saeed shouted after him but Karim ignored him.

Chapter Sixteen

Saeed summoned Kim to his home office the following day. She assumed that he wanted to chat about Amare's progress. After all, Amare had informed her about how much his father was invested in his studies. She went with nothing but praises on her mind. Amare was a hard working young man and his father needed to hear how well he was doing.

One of Saeed's maids ushered Kim into his office. Walking in, she found him scribbling away at some papers. Waiting for him to lift his head, she was unsure if she should sit down, so she remained standing as he continued with what he was doing.

Looking around, she found his office much like Karim's but it felt darker, colder and more oppressive. Growing impatient, she coughed, but he continued to shuffle his papers. Finally, she spoke up.

"Good afternoon, sheik," she said to him.

"Please have a seat, Miss Atkins," he said waving to the chair nearest her. Kim nodded and sat down opposite the sheik as he finished with his notes. She counted to ten in her head and then counted to ten four more times before he finally put his pen down and looked up at her.

"You wanted to see me?"

"I did indeed." Saeed studied her for a moment. He had so much displeasure on his face that Kim wondered what he was thinking about. "So, you are sleeping with my son," he said at last. Kim's eyes flew open. She had not been expecting that at all.

"Excuse me?" Kim had only slept with Karim once, and even if she was, that was not Saeed's business. Why was he asking her that and how had he found out?

"I know all about it and I must say that I am disappointed."

Kim knew that she was not the woman for Karim but she did not expect his father to get involved. Besides, they had only slept together once even if she did relive it over and over each night before bed.

"I do not understand, sir," she said, even though she did. She just did not know what to say to him.

"You are smart a girl. I am sure you understand my words," Saeed said, his lips tight. "I need you to distance yourself from my son."

Kim's jaw hung open. "I don't understand... why? I mean him no harm." Saeed dismissed her with his hand.

"Listen, Miss Atkins, Karim is my eldest son and he will marry a full Arabic woman and bear me grandchildren appropriate to my station."

"While I can understand your desire for grandchildren, it is Karim's choice who he wants to be with."

Saeed looked at her as if she was mad. "I do not care what you think; I will not have you poison my son against me."

Poison Karim against his father? This was simply ridiculous. Kim almost laughed because that was how stupid the sheik was sounding. "I would never turn your son against you."

"If you truly care for him, then you will leave him at once."

She did care for him. More than she had yet to admit to herself. What had started as a little crush, had soon developed into much more than that. She had tried her best not to fall for him but she failed miserably.

"Sheik Sharqi, I cannot see what I have done to offend you," Kim said calmly.

The sheik sighed. "I see, you won't leave easily." Saeed opened the drawer of his desk and pulled out a chequebook. He picked up his pen, clicked it and started writing out a cheque. He tore it out and passed it to Kim. She frowned as she picked it up. He had written her a cheque for fifty thousand dollars. She gasped.

"Why are you giving me money?" she asked. She really hoped he wasn't buying her off. It was insulting.

"I will give you this money if you agree to leave Karim alone and return to the states." He said calmly as if he was speaking wise words. This was all just business to him. Kim was disgusted at how cruelly his father was behaving.

"I do not want your money," Kim replied as she returned the cheque.

"I see, you want more money." He wrote out another cheque for one hundred thousand dollars. "Is this enough?" he asked her.

"Sheik, I do not want your money. Please keep it."

"Is this not enough? You western women are all so materialistic."

Kim was growing increasingly furious that he was generalising western women who were not all the same. She certainly was not materialistic. No matter how much money Saeed was going to offer, she was not going to take it.

If he were not much older than she was, she probably would have slapped him across the face. Sadly, he was old enough to be her father, and she was taught to respect her elders.

"I resent the fact that you think all western women are the same. Please keep your money; I do not want a dime of it."

"I know that you want more money. Stop pretending not to and take it. You are wasting my time." Saeed was getting agitated and impatient.

"I think I will leave now." Kim could no longer sit there and continue such a pointless conversation. She stood up and Saeed rose along with her.

"You do not leave until I tell you to," he shouted and banged his fist on his desk.

Looking at him, she backed slowly toward the door, "I am sorry; sir, but I will not continue this conversation with you. I will happily leave you."

"You spoilt American brat! You are so stubborn and disrespectful. I wish I had never hired you. You only came here to seduce my son and poison him with your western ways!" he shouted.

Staring at him, Kim's back bumped against the door as she reached around with her hand to find the handle. Not wanting to turn her back on him, she managed to open the door and slide out, shutting it behind her. Closing her eyes, she took deep breaths as she fought the urge to cry.

The man was completely insane; she thought as she walked quickly back to her quarters glad that she didn't run into anyone. As she walked, she thought about all the things that she wanted to say to him but she knew that if she did, she would only somehow be proving him right.

She burst into tears as soon as she walked into her room. Was it so wrong for her to love Karim? It was 2015 for goodness sake. All the bullshit about races not mixing should have died years ago. To Saeed, she was not good enough to be with his son because she was not Arabic. Taking a shuddering breath, she realised that there was no hope for a relationship with Karim if his father was so adamantly opposed to her.

Kim flipped open her suitcase and began throwing her clothes in. She had to get out of that house as fast as her legs could carry her. If Saeed did not want her around, she was going to leave as quickly and as quietly as possible. While she would miss both Amare and Karim, no job or relationship was worth putting up with that man.

Chapter Seventeen

Amare was in his study room preparing for his English exam when he heard voices coming from his father's office. His study was positioned between his father's and Karim's. When he heard the voices, he picked up a glass beaker and went to eavesdrop; the way he had seen Kim do. He listened to the entire conversation as he wondered how his father had found out about Karim and Kim in the first place.

He was shocked at what he had heard from his father's office. He could not believe that his father disliked Kim being with Karim that much. Amare was aware of how traditional his father was but he did not think that he would try to pay her off.

Amare knew that Kim did not deserve to be treated that way. He waited for a few moments after he had heard her leave his father's office before he went to speak with him.

Saeed was in the middle of venting to his friend, Kareef, when Amare walked in. Amare looked at Kareef and then at his father.

"Father, may I have a word?"

"Not now," Saeed snapped.

"It has to be right now."

"What is so important that it cannot wait?"

"I overheard your conversation with Kim." Amare was not that bothered that Kareef was in there as he was his father's closest friend and knew his personal business. He probably already knew about them.

"That does not concern you."

"Father, I think you are being too harsh."

Saeed looked at Amare as if he had lost his mind. Kareef just raised his eyebrows.

"Are all my sons bent on disobeying me now? All because of a mere woman?" Saeed laughed sarcastically.

"It is not that I am here to disobey you. I simply think that you are being too harsh. Kim has done nothing wrong."

"Given how quickly your sons jump to her defence, it seems that this Kim is special," Kareef commented as he looked at his old friend.

"She really is. She is a great tutor and a great person. Ever since she moved in, Karim has been much happier," Amare answered Kareef.

"If Karim loves her, given that he is your son, I do not see him readily giving her up," Kareef replied, hoping that his friend would see reason.

"That is why she must leave," Saeed demanded.

"Father that makes no sense; she is the best thing that has ever happened to him. Why on earth would you want him to give that up?"

"She is a western woman!"

"So what? Times have changed."

"I know." Saeed sighed and fell back in his chair. After a long few minutes he finally spoke. "This world is changing fast and I do not know how to handle it."

Amare raised his eyebrows. He'd never expected his father to say something like that. He had been fuming when Kim left his office. Kareef looked at Amare. Even he was shocked at Saeed's sudden change of mood.

"There is nothing you can do to stop the world from changing. You just have to accept it," Amare said. Saeed looked up at him.

"Is Karim really happy around her?" he asked.

"Yes, father, he really is. He is a different man; he is the better version of himself."

Kareef laughed, "I never thought I would see the day that Karim changes because of a woman." Amare agreed. He had never thought he would see that day too.

Amare first teased Kim about Karim when he saw her watching him working out in the courtyard. He later saw Karim stealing glances at her when he thought that she wasn't looking.

Whenever she was around him, even though he was not talking to her, he seemed happier. He had even taken her advice and computerised their accounting system because of her recommendation. The old him would have never listened to her.

"I never thought I would see that day either," Saeed replied.

"So, will you allow Kim to stay and be with Karim? Who knows, they might not work out but shouldn't they be at least given the opportunity to try?" Saeed was silent for a few moments.

"Fine," he said at last, exhaling loudly.

"What? You are really going to agree?" Kareef asked in shock. Saeed's reputation preceded him. Everyone knew how traditional and rigid he was. He even had problems with the Tazeems because of it.

He had strongly disliked Adilah Tazeem for her western ways. She may have been born of Arabic blood but she behaved like a westerner, which had made Saeed's blood boil. He had always expressed how grateful he was that she was not his daughter.

"Yes," Saeed nodded. "He refused to part ways with her. She also refused, no matter how much money I offered her."

"Father, offering her money to leave Karim was just wrong."

"I am aware of that."

"How much did you offer her?" Kareef asked her. Amare and Saeed both looked at him as if he was crazy. "I am just curious," he told them as he shrugged his shoulders.

"One hundred thousand," Saeed said quietly.

"You're worth hundreds of millions. Is that all you could offer her?" Kareef demanded.

"This isn't a situation to joke about."

"Even in your attempts to buy her off, you are still stingy," Kareef told him as he laughed. Saeed narrowed his gaze at him and Amare shook his head. Even he was smart enough to know that it was too early to joke about it. "Anyway, now that you are going to let her stay, I suppose you should go have a word with her."

"I guess so."

"And offer an apology. It is the right thing to do," Amare added.

Saeed rose from his seat. "This woman must be an angel. I have never seen you and your brother defend one person so much."

"She is an amazing person and she deserves it."

Saeed nodded. He left his office and headed to Kim's room. He had lost to both his sons. It was only right that he went to apologise to her for his inconsiderate and rude behaviour. He hoped that she would accept and agree to stay.

When Saeed reached her room, this time he knocked before he entered. The last thing he wanted was to see his naked son splayed across her bed again. Saeed walked into her room, but Kim was nowhere to be found. He quickly searched the room before calling out to the maid.

"Where is Miss Atkins?" he asked her. The maid bowed her head before she spoke.

"Sir, Miss Atkins has left the residence with her luggage." the maid replied.

Chapter Eighteen

Kim rushed out of the Sharqi residence as fast as her clumsy legs could carry her. Saeed's words kept echoing in her head and she knew that she had to leave that place immediately or risk saying something that she would regret. When she saw all those zeros on that cheque, a thousand thoughts ran through her mind.

She felt insulted. That was all Saeed saw her as; a materialistic woman that could be bought off just like that. It showed that Saeed did not believe that Kim had genuine feelings for Karim even though she truly cared for him and only wanted what was best for him.

For a split second, part of her considered taking the money and using it to keep the orphanage open. Those girls had nowhere else to go and the money would have gone a long way toward securing their futures.

She felt bad for considering the money but it was for a good cause. She was also unclear about how Karim felt about her. Maybe she was fighting a losing battle. Either way, she knew that if she took that money, then there was never going to be any hope for them.

As Kim was pulling her suitcase toward the car, she bumped into something and almost lost her balance. She looked up and saw Karim standing in front of her. "Where's the fire?" he asked her.

"Sorry," she apologised.

"Where are you off to? You stood me up when I asked you to meet me in your room."

"I did not mean to." Kim tucked her hair behind her ear in agitation.

"I waited and waited for you."

Kim raised her eyebrows and then looked at the ground. When she had finally made it back to her room, he wasn't there. She had not realised that he waited for her. She wished that she had gone to him as they could have enjoyed their last moments together before she left.

"I didn't realise. I was prepping Amare and his friends for their exam," she said quietly. Karim moved closer to her and touched her waist.

"Never mind, the damage is already done now. How will you make it up to me?" he asked her. The feeling of his hand on her waist made her shatter inside. She knew that she would never feel his touch again. She so badly wanted to walk into his arms and just cry on his chest.

"I am afraid I cannot make it up to you. You'll have to forgive me," she told him unable to look him in the eyes.

"You have to. You cannot leave me hanging like that and not try to make it up to me." Karim pulled Kim closer and kissed her on the cheek expecting her to melt in his arms. While she would have liked nothing better, it made her realise how much she was going to miss him.

"You are quiet today," Karim said. "What is the matter?"

"I am going back home, Karim."

"Home? What do you mean?" Karim looked down and saw the suitcase next to her. He looked back at her waiting for an answer.

"I am going back to the States. Your father does not want me around you, and he is right. We could never work."

"I don't understand. Why would you suddenly leave without talking to me first?"

"I was never going to stay here forever anyway. It's best that I return now before we do something that we will both regret."

"Kimberly, you are not making any sense!"

"Amare has learned a great deal. He will be fine without me here."

"And what about me? Will I be fine without you here?"

Kim fought back the tears. She wished that she could stay there with him but she could not. He would soon find someone more appropriate to his status.

"You will be fine. We would have never worked anyway."

"What does that mean? We would not have worked?" Karim placed his hands on his hips and waited for her response. Kim reached out and touched his face for the last time.

"We are too different. You are Arabic and I am not. You are a sheik, and I am a clumsy school teacher," she said to him as she bit her lip to keep from crying.

"So what?" he asked.

"I am just a *spoilt American brat*. We can never be together, Karim." Kim caressed his cheek with the back of her hand and then walked off leaving Karim standing there speechless, as his father's words played in his head.

Chapter Nineteen

Karim watched Kim get into the car. He knew that he had been remiss in not sharing his feelings with her, but in truth, until he had lashed out at his father, he didn't know how he felt about her and now, it may be too late. No, it can't be too late! She was needed here. Amare still needed her to get him through his studies. And he needed her, at his side.

She had said that they were too different and it would have never worked. He liked the fact that she was different from all the women he had ever been with. He found her smart, funny and when she smiled at him, the whole room lit up.

A spoilt American brat. The words echoed in his head. That was what his father called her. Karim frowned as he remembered their argument. He suddenly realised that his father had something to do with her sudden departure. Nothing else made sense.

The sound of the car's engine snapped him out of his thoughts as he watche the car moving swiftly out of the driveway and Kim, out of his life forever.

"*Khara!*" Karim swore in Arabic. He started running after the car but it was too far away. "Kim!" he shouted as he ran after the car. It was right there in front of him. She only needed to hear him calling her name.

He dropped to his knees. This was it. Kim was gone and he had lost her.

Karim heard the sound of a car behind him. "Karim!" It was Amare's voice. He turned his head and saw his brother and father pull up in a car. "Get in!" Amare shouted as Karim jumped to his feet.

Running around to the side of the car, he pulled open the door and slid into the backseat as his father put his foot on the gas before he had the door shut. Holding on, he reached for his seatbelt as he caught his father's eye in the rear view mirror.

"This is my fault and I plan to fix this," his father told him as he drove.

Holding tight to the side of the car, Karim couldn't remember the last time his father drove as he always had a driver to take him places. He coughed to mask his yelp when his father hit a large pothole.

"Sorry, didn't see it," his father said cheerfully as he smacked his hand on the car horn and swerved around slower cars as the drivers waved their fists in anger. Waving merrily at them, "Truth be told, I haven't had this much fun in decades," he commented as he laughed. The brothers looked at each other in shock wondering who this strange man was masquerading as their father.

"Taleb is not going to believe this," Amare said over his shoulder as they bounced over another pothole.

"What won't Taleb believe?" Saeed asked as he turned to look at his son.

"Father, the road!" Karim called out in alarm as Saeed quickly straightened out the wheel.

"My son, I was driving long before you were born," his father chastised him as he drove.

"Yes, but now the cars have engines," Amare shot back as his father turned to glare at him. "Watch the road," Amare called out in alarm as he tightened his hold on his seatbelt.

Taking the next rise a bit too fast, the car bounced heavily on the asphalt as the airport came into view. As his father sped down the hill, they could see that all the gates already had planes waiting for passengers.

"Which one is it?" Karim asked as he worried that the plane would take off before they get there.

Tapping at his phone, Amare found which flight was taking off for the States as he pointed the plane out. "That one!" he shouted as his father drove toward the runway.

"Father, the parking lot is that way," Karim pointed out as his father kept driving.

"Look!" his father pointed. "The passengers are already walking to the plane. We won't make it if we park the car." Speeding up, he began wildly honking the horn as he headed for the service gate. A guard came out and was madly waving his arms, but Saeed sped up and crashed through the barrier as the guard dove for cover. "Send me the bill," he shouted out the window at the frightened guard.

Driving toward the plane, Saeed finally slowed down as the car rolled to a stop. Leaping out of the car, the brothers ran toward the passengers calling out Kim's name.

"Kim Atkins!" they shouted. "Kimberly Atkins!"

As the passengers turned to stare at the two men, they finally saw her head pop out from inside the plane, as she stared at them dumbfounded.

"Kim! Kim!" Amare shouted. "You must come down here!"

The passengers stepped aside in bemusement as Kimberly slowly walked down the stairs toward the brothers who were laughing and clapping each other on the back.

Chapter Twenty

"What are you doing here?" she whispered unsure if her voice would be steady if she spoke in a normal tone. Many of the passengers had pulled out their phones and were taking videos of them.

Karim walked towards her and took her hands in his. Kissing them both, he looked into her eyes, "Don't go," he said simply. Kim gasped and stared at him. She did not know what to say or to do. She just stood there wide-eyed staring at him.

"Don't go back, not now. Not before we've had a chance to see if we will work." Looking at her face, he realised that she had been crying and his face softened as he rubbed her cheek. "Please stay. At least for a little while longer," he pleaded.

In her heart, Kim wanted to say yes, but she needed answers.

"But your father…"

"Is an old fool who needs someone like you around to remind him what it's like to be young and in love," Saeed said as he walked around the side of the car toward her.

Shaking her head, Kim rubbed her eyes and looked back up, as Saeed grinned at her. "Yes, even an old dog like me can mend his ways."

Suddenly remembering what he had just said, she looked at Karim, "Love?"

Nodding his head, Karim looked at her, "Love."

Staring at him, Kim still couldn't comprehend what was going on. "So, you, love me?" she asked.

Nodding his head again, "Yes, I love you, Kimberly Atkins."

Shaking her head, Kim stepped back wondering if this was some sort of cruel joke. How could he love her? Realizing that she didn't believe him, he stepped toward the passengers who had clustered around them to watch.

Pointing to her, he looked at them, "Evidently, she doesn't believe me," he told them as they nodded in agreement. "I seem to have a reputation as someone who was adamant that love did not exist. That love was for the weak." Clutching his hands to his heart, he looked at Kim, "Well, if that is the case, then I can think of no better woman to lose myself to than Miss Atkins over there."

Wiping the tears off her face, she still refused to walk to him. "You don't believe in relationships."

Waving his finger in the air, he looked at the passengers again. "Now that was once true. Like love, I thought that relationships made you weak because it would mean depending on someone else. But it also means that they will stand by your side through the good *and* the bad. Unfortunately, I find that I am in love with the one woman who isn't eager to jump my bones," he told them conspiratorially. "What am I going to do about that?" he asked.

"Incoming!" Amare shouted moments before he felt Kimberly slam into his back sending them both tumbling to the ground.

Rolling onto his back to catch her, he laughed as she joyously kissed his face.

"I love you too, Karim Sharqi," she shouted as the passengers began to clap and cheer.

The sound of sirens in the distance had Saeed Sharqi looking over his shoulder.

"Oh dear, I think those are for me," he said calmly.

"Wait, what?" Kim asked.

Laughing, "Yes, father crashed through the security barrier so we wouldn't miss your flight," Amare told her.

"So, if you don't mind, could we please keep an old man out of jail and get out of here?" Saeed asked plaintively as everyone laughed. "Come on, I'll drive," he offered as he walked toward the driver's side.

"No!" the brothers shouted in unison.

Chapter Twenty-one

Two months later, Kim sat in the courtyard with Saeed; teaching him how to use a computer as he eagerly scoured the current news feeds for stock information. He chuckled with glee over a human-interest piece about him saving the orphanage.

Karim stood at a distance and watched her tutoring his father. It was crazy how things had changed so much in such a short time. Six months ago, he was working out right there in the courtyard while Kim had been spying on him from above. He had known that she was watching him from the moment she rustled the curtains and he had stayed out there far longer than he normally would. So much so, that he was sore the next day, but it was worth it.

While he would not have readily admitted his attraction to her, it pleased him that she found him desirable more than any other woman had and it had taken him months finally to understand why. Without intending to, she had managed to get under his skin in ways that no other human had ever done and now, he couldn't imagine it any other way.

***

The last two months had been very eventful for Kim. She was actually spending time with Saeed and teaching him how to use the computer. Kim and Saeed slowly built a relationship as she worked to show him that not all western women were bad.

Thankfully, he came to realise his mistake and even told Kim that she was good for Karim. He had changed for the better because of her. Amare had also passed his exams with flying colours and was amongst the top ten in the country.

Saeed was so grateful to Kim for Amare's high marks that he had offered her a large bonus, but instead of taking the cheque, she asked him to save the orphanage instead. Her response caught Saeed off guard, as he didn't expect her to be so generous. Picking up the phone, he called the director to find out exactly how much they needed and he readily agreed to cover all their financial needs.

"I believe I misjudged you gravely," he told her as he read the article about the orphanage. She smiled and shook her head.

"That is all in the past now," she said to him, pressing her hand into his.

"I am glad that we have this second chance to get to know one another."

Kim was also pleased to have the opportunity to know Saeed. Even though he was a strict and traditional man, deep down he cared for his sons and wanted what was best for them. In the last two months, he had showed Kim kindness and he saved the orphanage.

"Me too. And, I am grateful for the donation you made. I can't begin to express how much it helped the girls who have no one else."

"It's alright, my dear. I am just touched by your actions. Most people would have taken the money for themselves."

Kim smiled. She looked around, wondering where Karim had disappeared. She was sitting in the very spot where she had seen him working out all those months ago and the thought of it made her smile, as she remembered how shocked she was when he winked at her.

The past two months with Karim had been great for Kim. She had really gotten to know him and found that he was unlike the man she thought he was. He was so caring and fun. She had never been so happy in her life. A part of her still worried that this was all some lavish dream and any moment, she would wake up.

Claire had teased her, telling her that she was never coming back. She honestly did not feel like returning. Life with Karim brought her joy and her volunteer work at the orphanage made her feel fulfilled. Amare walked out onto the courtyard.

"Hello all," he said as he sat down at the table. He picked up Kim's glass and drank her iced tea.

"Amare!" she chastised. "I was still drinking that."

"Thanks, I was really thirsty," he said with a cheeky grin and put the glass down on the table. Kim frowned at him.

"I did not give it to you," she told him before she hit his shoulder in mock anger. Saeed just laughed and shook his head.

Suddenly they heard the warning alarm for a coming sand storm. Looking at each other, they quickly rose and walked inside. Realising that the alarm was coming from in the house, instead of outside, they followed the sound around to the entryway where they came upon some of the girls from the orphanage standing there holding letters to form a sentence.

They all smiled at her as they held their letters up. Kim read the sentence aloud, "Will… you… marry… me?"

Karim was standing with them. He walked towards Kim and dropped to one knee as he took her left hand in his.

"Kimberly Atkins, will you make me the happiest man alive and marry me?" he asked her. Pulling a velvet box out of his pocket, he opened it and presented it to her. Kim gasped when she saw the huge blue sapphire mounted on a platinum band. There were tiny diamonds around the sapphire that twinkled in the sunlight.

"Yes," she said to him as she wiggled her fingers impatiently while he slid the ring on. "Of course, I will marry you." Rising to his feet, he swept her up into his arms and kissed her deeply as everyone cheered

Epilogue

"Karim, I have to go," Kim complained. She had to go to the orphanage but Karim was not allowing her to get out of bed. Since they had been engaged, she had spent every night in his bed.

"Stay a bit longer," he whispered against her ear before he nibbled on it making her giggle.

"I already stayed an hour longer than I should have."

He caressed her back as he stroked his way down toward her ass. Kim quickly jumped out of bed. She knew that once he started touching her, there would be no end to it. She would never be able to get out of bed and they would spend the whole day in together. Again. She rushed out of his room and back to her own. She had enough time to take a quick shower and get to the orphanage.

"Kim! Over here!" Salma signalled for her. Kim rushed over to the other teachers.

"Hey guys, I am running late."

"Don't worry there is someone taking over your class already."

Kim frowned. "Who?" she asked. She always looked forward to teaching her girls.

"That does not matter. You've been the talk of the orphanage this week," Dania told her.

"Let's see the ring." Rene said to her. Kim giggled as she held her hand out to the women. "It's massive."

"It's so gorgeous. You're so lucky," Salma told her.

"I'm jealous," Dania told her.

"So, I ask again, how is it living with Karim Sharqi?" Dania asked her as the ladies all giggled together. Feeling her phone vibrate, Kim fished it out of her purse. It was a message from Claire. It was her first week working in the library at Harvard and Kim was excited to find out how she was doing. The message read:

You won't believe who I just saw...

END OF BOOK ONE

Thank You!

Thank you so much for purchasing, downloading and reading my book. It's hard for me to put into words how much I appreciate my readers. If you enjoyed it, please remember to leave a review for it. I love hearing from my readers! I want to keep you guys happy :). For all books by Leslie North go to:

Leslie North's Amazon Page

OR Visit Her Website: LeslieNorthBooks.com

Get FIVE full-length, highly-rated Leslie North Novellas FREE! Sign-up to her mailing list and start reading them within minutes:

http://leslienorthbooks.com/sign-up-for-free-books/

The Botros Brothers Series (Exclusively on Kindle Unlimited)

The Sheik's Accidental Pregnancy **(EXCERPT BELOW)**

The Sheik's Defiant Girlfriend

The Sheikh's Demanding Fiancée

The Sheikha's Determined Police Officer

The Jawhara Sheiks Series

The Sheik's Pregnant Bride (FREE)

The Sheik's Troublesome Bride

The Sheik's Captive Bride

The Fedosov Family Series

The Russian's Stubborn Lover (FREE)

The Russian's Bold American

The Russian's Secret Child

The Denver Men Series

The CEO's Pregnant Lover

The Marine's Virgin Lover

FBI Agent's Reluctant Lover

Navy Seal's Innocent Italian

It was finally Friday, the last day of the workweek and the last late work night! Sara was happy. She was not used to working such late nights and it was exhausting. She could not wait to get the work over and done with so that she could start her weekend, kick back and relax.

She had worked with Amir every night and he laughed at how tired she got. He kept saying that she was too cute. Sara never understood how she was cute but it didn't bother her. That Friday, Amir had a mysterious appointment he needed to go to. Sara manned his appointments and she was unaware of this one.

"Sir, you're being too secretive," she said to him as he laughed and ruffled her hair.

"I am not," he replied.

"Then, why do I not know about this appointment?

And why aren't I coming along?"

"You're working late," Amir replied as he kept inching towards the door. Sara placed her hands on her hips and stared at him.

"A date?" Sara asked him.

"I shall see you on Monday," Amir smiled mischievously. Sara laughed and bid him farewell. She knew that he was going on a date. He seemed to be quite the ladies' man. She made a mental note to grill him about him it on Monday. She took the files she needed from his desk and locked his door before she headed back to her office.

After what seemed like hours and hours of work, Sara decided to walk around the building. After sitting for so long, she needed to stretch and relax for a bit. The place was deserted so she kicked off her shoes before wandering around. Sara frowned as she wished that she were home or out with the twins.

Sara dragged her feet as she walked around the building. She didn't even care what she looked like, nobody was there to see her. She was wearing a black knee-length, pencil skirt and a white camisole that she had untucked. Her long curly hair had long ago come loose from its bun, so she left it down as it rested on her back.

She turned a corner and saw the light on in the conference room. She growled silently. Who had not bothered to switch the light off? She dragged her feet and headed towards the conference room to switch the light off. She walked into the room and towards the light switch. She was in her own world looking at the ground.

"Can I help you with something?" A deep voice sounded from behind her. It startled her as she squealed and turned around quickly.

"Oh gosh," she sighed with relief. It was Tariq leaning on the table reading some paperwork. He was wearing grey pants and a white shirt. A couple of buttons were unbuttoned, revealing the top of his chest. "You scared me," she scolded.

"Do you need something?" he asked her. Sara shrugged. She didn't really expect him to be polite to her.

"I saw the light on and I came to switch it off because I thought no one was in here," Sara replied. Tariq stared at her. She looked untidy and she was barefoot!

"Why are you barefoot?" He could not help himself. He had to ask her.

"I was wearing heels all day. My feet hurt," Sara responded in an unfriendly tone. She was trying her best not to snap at him but she had lost her patience with his attitude long ago. He did not respond to her as he stared at her. "Working late?" she asked. She caught his gaze and suddenly felt uncomfortable as she slowly inched for the door. He didn't respond to her as he felt like she was asking an obvious question. Sara placed her hands on her hips.

"Why is it that you can never answer me or even act polite towards me?" Sara asked him. She couldn't ignore it anymore. He always felt the need to be that way towards her and she had not done anything to him. On top of that, she was tired and had enough of his attitude towards her.

Tariq raised his eyebrows as he regarded her. He was not expecting her to question him nor did she have the right to. "I am not obligated to do either," he said. His voice was now deeper.

"I never did anything to offend you."

She has full lips, Tariq thought to himself as he remembered her licking her lips in the restaurant. It did not matter anyway he thought. "Your persona is offensive," he said to her.

"Excuse me?"

"Who walks around barefoot?"

Sara frowned. *You're the one with an ugly persona.* She looked away. She was in the middle of arguing with him and his chest was distracting her. From the little glimpse she got, she could tell that he was very toned. The bulk of his muscles were always showing in the clothes he wore and how was it that he had time to exercise when he was always working?

"You do not act like a lady should," Tariq added.

"I am good at my job and that's all you should be concerned about," Sara shot back.

"For England, perhaps. But this is Saudi Arabia and you work for the Botros."

"Because you're so freaking special," Sara mumbled under her breath as she headed for the door. If she stayed in there any longer, she would say things that she would regret. She liked Amir and respected him enough not to disrespect his brother. She got the shock of her life when

Tariq grabbed her arm and pulled her back.

"What did you say?" he demanded. He had pulled her close to him and she was now standing inches from him. She was shocked at how he pulled her so easily as if she weighed nothing.

"Being a little bit more polite and less judgemental to others will not harm you," Sara said. She was not going to let him intimidate her; she was going to stand her ground. His gaze had grown darker and more intense. He stared at her and she stared back. She was not going to look away first.

"You think you can speak to me any way you wish?"

"Unhand me."

"If I don't?"

Exactly, what will I do if he does not let go off me?

"Try it and find out." An empty threat. There was nothing she could do. He called her bluff keeping his hand on her sending tingles up her arm. Instead, he pulled her even closer to him. Sara landed between his legs and her hands landed on his chest. His face was now inches away from his. Wow, he smells good, why is it she hadn't noticed his cologne before? It was intoxicating on him.

"Time to make good on your threat," he said to her as he stared at her lips.

"Please let go," she whispered. She knew that she needed to get out of there. Something unexpected was happening and she wasn't prepared.

Tariq let go of her arm but Sara didn't move. She felt paralysed. She so badly wanted to flee from the room but her legs failed her. Tariq wrapped one arm around her waist and pulled her closer to him. Her whole body was now flush against his as both palms rested on his rock hard chest. Without waiting, he planted a kiss on her lips as her eyes widened in surprise.

He gently kissed her and she did not stop him. Her mind went blank. She could not think about anything. As she gasped, he gently pushed his tongue into her mouth and deepened the kiss. Sara wrapped her arms around his neck and kissed him back. His hands stroked her back. He broke the kiss. Sara was breathing hard and still had her eyes closed.

"What are you doing?" she whispered.

"What are you?" he asked the question back.

He pressed a feather-light kiss on her neck, which sent ripples of sensation all over her body. She let out a soft moan as she shuddered against him. He continued to kiss her neck as Sara rubbed his back and dug her nails into his flesh.

Before she knew it, her skirt was on the floor and Tariq was caressing and squeezing her bottom. She did not like this man but her senses had left her. She should put a stop to it, but he was doing things to her insides that she'd only ever read about.

Excerpt From The Sheikh's Accidental Pregnancy (The Botros Brothers Series Book 1)

Printed in Great Britain
by Amazon

56003719R00098